HARVESTING MOONSHINE
& OTHER STORIES

HARVESTING MOONSHINE
& OTHER STORIES

By M.L.D. CURELAS

TYCHE BOOKS LTD.

Published by Tyche Books Ltd.
Calgary, Alberta, Canada
www.TycheBooks.com

Cover Design by Indigo Chick Designs
Interior Layout by M.L.D. Curelas

Tyche Books Ltd Edition 2025
Print ISBN: 978-1-989407-88-2
Ebook ISBN: 978-1-989407-89-9

For Aunt Helen
and
Jason
for always believing

TABLE OF CONTENTS

INTRODUCTION

Hope. I was surprised when I re-read these stories that hope was a recurring theme. A belief that something better is on the horizon, that situations can improve, that growth and change are possible. Hand in hand with hope are collaboration, teamwork, and friendship: we can do anything together.

Hope is one of "those lovely intangibles" that Doris and Fred argue about in *Miracle on 34th Street*. You can't see it, can't touch it, can't buy it, but if you don't have it, you're miserable. Hope makes life worth living.

Hope is hard to hang onto right now, with war, economic hardships, and deteriorating human rights dominating the news and political discourse. So, here. From me to you, a collection of hope—bundled in fantastic tales of science fiction and steampunk and space operas.

While I write all kinds of speculative fiction, this collection focuses on my science fiction; you'll find tales with a retro feel—set in classic works of science fiction or engaging with historical events or people. You'll also find a lot of "punk" tales: steampunk (stories set in an alternate Victorian-era, with steam-powered machines), dieselpunk (tales set in an alternate WWI – 1950s), and one story I'm calling librarypunk.

I've resisted the urge to revise the stories. Some are well over a decade old, but they are important stepping-stones in my writing career, so I've let them alone, other than fixing typos and punctuation errors. All of the stories, regardless of age, contain a nugget of hope, sparkling and gritty.

M.L.D. Curelas
Calgary, March 2025

HARVESTING MOONSHINE

Originally published in *49th Parallels*, edited by Hayden Trenholm. Bundoran Press, 2017.

The kick-off story. The submissions call for 49th Parallels asked for alternate Canadian histories and timelines, and I loved the challenge of creating an alternate history involving one of my favourite physicists, Lord Rutherford, who did some of his notable work on radioactivity at McGill University. Writing more stories in this alternate Canada is on my to-do list; Hazel is a lot of fun to write.

HARUESTING MOONSHINE

"Anyone who looked for a source of power in the transformation of the atoms was talking moonshine." — Lord Ernest Rutherford, Father of Nuclear Physics, 1933

Hazel stared at the telegram. Sister Ruth sick Stop Need you home Stop Flight 2100 Stop

They were calling her back? After all the work put into creating her false US Army personnel file and ID? Getting her stationed at this base in the middle of nowhere? She couldn't leave tonight. She had made meticulous plans for next week, when her temporary assignment at the base finished. All of her months of hard work, for nothing. Hazel's hands clenched into fists, crumpling the telegram. She chucked it at the trash can.

"Bad news, Private Wilkes?"

Hazel let her hands drop to her lap as she swivelled in her chair. "My sister is ill, sir, and my . . . brother wants me to come home tonight."

Colonel Barnes stood in the doorway to the inner office, holding several folders. Tall and broad, he had droopy eyes and sagging cheeks and reminded Hazel of a basset hound. "Home?" His eyebrows arched. "Must be serious if they're calling you back to . . . New York, isn't it?"

"Yes, sir," she responded automatically, before she recalled her cover story and added, "But it's Vermont, sir, not New York."

"Vermont, of course." He glanced at the clock. "I need you to stay late tonight."

"But my brother has already arranged a flight," she said.

Barnes dropped the stack of folders on her desk. "The Canadians have turned down another uranium purchase request. Their damned new Prime Minister and his notions of peace." He scowled. "I have letters that need to be sent off tomorrow."

Hazel forced a smile. "Coffee during dictation, sir?"

"Sounds wonderful, Private, thank you."

Hazel glared at the stack of folders until the colonel's door clicked shut. Recalled from her mission and now stuck working late. It was hard to imagine her evening getting worse. "Better start the coffee," she muttered, pushing away from the desk. As she measured out grounds, she considered the telegram again. Flight at 9 pm seemed obvious. So did "Need you home"—she was to return to Chalk River. But "Sister Ruth sick?" Ruth was what they called Lord Rutherford, but as he'd passed away several years ago, still in harness at eighty-four, he certainly wasn't sick. And her circle of female physicist friends called themselves the Ruths, but that was several people, not an individual.

As the coffee percolated merrily, Hazel started filing the folders. Maybe Ruth did refer to an individual. Sylvia, perhaps? Would she be pulled off this mission to take over Sylvia's medical research? Hazel slid the last file into the cabinet and sighed. It was infuriating to abandon the mission early. She'd cultivated a promising sergeant, one of the security guards.

The coffee machine burbled to a stop as the last few drops fell into the pot. Hazel prepared a cup for the colonel, her unfocused gaze resting on the coat tree tucked into the corner of the office for several seconds before registering what she was seeing. Her green canvas messenger bag peeped out from underneath her coat.

Hazel put the cup and saucer on a tray, added two cookies, and carried the tray to her desk. Glancing at the colonel's door, Hazel removed the bag from its hook. Scuffed, with frayed edges, the bag was unremarkable on the outside. The interior, however, personally customized, was quite unusual. Several pouches and loops containing tools were sewn into the supple leather lining. She could salvage the mission. Everything she needed was in those pouches.

She replaced the bag, retrieved a notepad and pencil, which she slipped into a jacket pocket, and grabbed the tray. "I am a happy, faithful secretary," she muttered, pasting another smile on her face. Balancing the tray on one arm, she let herself into the colonel's office.

"Coffee, sir," Hazel said, placing the tray on his desk. Pulling out the notepad and pencil from her pocket, she sat in the chair at the corner of the colonel's desk.

Barnes sipped his coffee. "You seem a good girl, Private, from what I've seen these past few weeks."

Hazel held her pencil poised above her notebook, cheeks starting to ache from keeping the smile on her face. "Thank you, sir?"

He nodded. "You've been seen out at the igloo a lot in the last few days."

"Oh!" Her smile relaxed. "Well . . ." Not able to blush on command, Hazel angled her face downwards and swept her eyes shut for a few seconds. She hoped she looked demure. "Sergeant Thomson, sir."

"Yes, Sergeant Thomson," Barnes said. "He has a reputation, Private Wilkes. If you want a successful military career, you'll need to control yourself."

"Yes, sir," Hazel murmured. She had no intention of not seeing Thomson before she left, of course. His reputation was useful, as was his shift schedule.

Barnes took another sip of his drink. "Let's do some of these letters. You can have a dinner break afterwards, and then we'll finish up. Don't want you to miss your flight tonight—you did say tonight, Private?"

"Yes, sir," she said. "2100 hours."

To her relief, Barnes stopped at only a few letters. She rattled them out quickly on the typewriter and stacked them neatly on the desk. She'd have the colonel sign them and prepare the envelopes after her break.

There was still coffee in the pot. She poured the remainder into her thermos and sweetened the brew to Thomson's taste. From an unlabelled bottle that she kept her in messenger bag, Hazel added a careful pinch of powder. She smirked. She wouldn't return to Chalk River unsuccessful.

With the thermos of doctored coffee dangling from one hand and the messenger bag slung across her shoulder, Hazel left the office. She had thirty minutes.

Sergeant Thomson had been expecting her; she didn't see any other guards.

"Good evening, Private Wilkes!" he said with a cheerful smile.

"I'm sorry for being late—the Old Man decided to work late tonight," she said, forcing a hint of breathlessness into her voice. She waggled the thermos. "I brought you some coffee."

He laughed. "You make the best coffee on the base. They should make you permanent staff."

That's what a PhD in physics will get you, she thought sourly. *The ability to make the perfect cup of coffee.* She ducked her head so he couldn't see the frown puckering her face, and unscrewed the cap of the thermos. Flipping it over, she filled the lid with steaming coffee.

"Thanks, Hazel," Thomson said, saluting her with the cup before raising it to his mouth.

Hazel caught him as he sagged, tugging the coffee cup out of his hands. She set him and the cup on the ground and checked her watch.

Twenty minutes.

Romancing guards had perks. Keys to secure areas was her favourite.

The storage igloo was silent. Cold. Creepy. Massive bombs loomed in the middle of the building, cradled in their racks. While not as large as Fat Man, the bomb that had been dropped on Nagasaki, the MK5 still weighed a few thousand pounds and was ugly as sin. Not for the first time, Hazel wished she'd been assigned the disarmament of Goose Air Base. A US base located within Canada seemed safer somehow than sneaking around an American army base in the middle of a US desert.

Hazel rolled her shoulders, pushing her anxiety away. She didn't have time for atmospheric, superstitious nonsense. She had nuclear bombs to disable.

She only had six neutron disruptors, so Hazel went down the first row and stopped at the sixth one in. She crouched beside the nose, where the plutonium pit was located. Reaching into her bag, she removed a device about the size of her wristwatch. She placed it on the underside of the bomb, sighing in relief when it attached with a quiet ting, and depressed the button.

She knew she wouldn't be able to hear anything, but she cocked her head anyway, hoping for a sign that the americium-beryllium reaction had been successfully triggered. After a few seconds, she straightened with a shake. She had helped design the disrupters, she knew that the bomb's plutonium pit was being bombarded with neutrons from the americium-beryllium disruptor. She knew that the neutron bombardment would trigger small fission reactions in the plutonium pit. The bomb would fizzle here, in the storage igloo, quietly burning away its plutonium. It would be useless for its intended purpose.

Hazel stood and hurried to the next bomb.

Ernest Rutherford had once decried atomic energy research as a quest for moonshine, but had devoted himself to the research after his near-death in 1937. He had eagerly joined the British and Canadian atomic bomb research team at the Montreal Laboratory—after all, he'd done some of his seminal research at McGill University and remained fond of the country in which he'd lived for several years. And, just as he had done at McGill, he'd welcomed female physicists and chemists to his research team. It had been a dream come true for Hazel when he'd accepted her application in the fall of 1944.

Only he hadn't been interested in developing bombs for the Americans. Able to visualize all too well the destructive power of atom-splitting, he'd left the Montreal lab for the nuclear research facilities at Chalk River in Ontario and convinced the Canadians to follow a different path, a path of power and leadership for after the war was won. One Canadian in particular had been interested in Rutherford's ideas: Lester "Mike" Pearson.

It was, Hazel reflected as she triggered her fourth neutron disruptor, a rewarding path. She'd worked with Lord Rutherford for years before his death. She'd worked alongside other women physicists, forming bonds and friendships that held true even now, separated as they were by duty. In addition to the disruptor design, she'd been part of the team that had developed the nuclear generator for the submarines that patrolled and secured the Arctic for Canada.

After his peacekeeping success with the Suez Crisis, Mike Pearson had focused on Canada, eventually persuading the hawks within the government to first limit and then halt uranium shipments to the US. Then, when his shocking upset over Diefenbaker in the 1958 general election granted him greater influence, Prime Minister Pearson decided to take his nuclear policies one step further, creating a clandestine Peacekeeping Force whose aim was to disarm bombs made with Canadian uranium.

With the unchecked nuclear proliferation of both the US and Russia, and Canada leery of being caught between the two, Pearson had been swarmed with volunteers. In the end, his covert disarmament team had female members only. As Hazel had discovered first-hand, no one suspected secretaries to have the least bit of scientific knowledge, let alone advanced degrees in physics and practical experience in handling fissile material.

The sixth disrupter engaged, Hazel glanced at her watch again. Five minutes. She hurried outside, locking the door behind her.

Thomson was still on the ground, but he was moaning and one leg kicked, stirring up clouds of dust. Hazel hurried to his side and knelt. She grabbed the coffee cup, splashed the contents on his shirt, and tossed the cup aside, letting it roll away. Tipping over the thermos so its tampered contents would soak into the dirt, she bit the inside of her cheek. As tears welled, she clasped Thomson's hand.

"Billy, are you okay?" She patted his wrist. "Oh, please wake up."

Thomson groaned. His eyelashes fluttered and his eyes cracked open. "Hazel?"

"Oh, Billy! You just fainted! What's wrong?"

He tried to lift his head. "I don't . . . know?"

Hazel helped him sit up. "Your coffee spilled all over. Does it burn?" She dabbed at the stain on his jacket with a handkerchief.

"No, but my head is killing me," he said, rubbing his temples.

"I couldn't catch you," Hazel lied.

"It's not your fault, Hazel," Thomson said. "You know, I don't even remember falling—or what we were doing before."

Hazel patted his hand again. "You must have had a big bump."

It took a few more minutes to settle Thomson. He would see the doctor—after his shift, being too embarrassed to let anyone know he'd fainted. As he hadn't eaten before his shift, he'd eagerly accepted Hazel's suggestion that his blood sugar had been too low.

Hazel slunk into her office. She was only a few minutes late. Maybe Barnes—

"Private Wilkes!"

Damn.

Hazel hung up her bag. Grabbing her notepad and pencil, she went into the inner office.

Barnes stood at the window, looking out—at nothing, she supposed. It was dark.

"All ready for your trip, Wilkes?"

"I have to finish up those letters, sir, and—"

He cut her off with an impatient wave. "No, no. Are you ready for your trip? I certainly hope you don't catch something from your . . . sister."

Hazel's mouth went dry. Sick. There wasn't a sister Ruth in their codes. But they called themselves the Ruths, unofficially. *You've been thick this evening, Hazel old girl.* "Sister Ruth" did refer to an individual. *She* was the sick one.

They knew about her.

Her fingers tightened around her pencil. "Well, not really, sir. It's so sudden, I still have to pack a bag."

Barnes turned from the window. "Did you know, Private Wilkes, that Canada didn't dedicate all their resources to aiding us during the War? Only some worked on the bomb research that we so desperately needed. Most worked on other projects."

Hazel shook her head, although of course she did know that, having been there. She tried not to think about the Rosenbergs.

"Now they're undisputed kings of the arctic, with those nuclear submarines, and refusing to sell us uranium," he said, sitting at his desk. "Did you know that about Canada, Private?"

She started to shake her head again, but paused, her gaze caught by Barnes' coffee cup. *I can use that.* Illness made most people uncomfortable, and Barnes was no exception. Hazel covered her mouth with one hand, pencil clattering to the floor. She clutched her stomach and doubled over. Face hidden, it was easy to insert a finger down her throat. She gagged, shoulders hunching, a hideous croak erupting from her mouth.

"Private!"

She heard hurried footsteps, but didn't look up, not even when Barnes placed a hand on her shoulder. She moaned.

"What's wrong, Private?" Barnes patted her shoulder.

Hazel drew in a ragged breath. "Coffee . . . I had coffee with Billy Thomson." She moaned again. "He fainted and . . . oh, my stomach."

"Coffee?" Barnes asked, alarmed. The hand left her shoulder. "Maybe you should see the medic."

"But . . . the letters." She moaned again.

"Go see the medic, Private Wilkes, that's an order. We'll finish our discussion later."

Hazel stifled a smile. Still doubled up, she shuffled out of Barnes' office, moaning every few seconds. Once the door shut behind her, she dropped her pad on the desk and gathered up her things. She shuffled out of the outer office, uttering another retching sound and a few more moans for Barnes' benefit.

Alone in the corridor, she straightened. It would take Barnes a few minutes to check up on her at the medic's office—he was probably anxiously sniffing his coffee cup right now. She didn't have much time to leave the base and get to the airport. Smiling, she patted her jacket pocket. Thomson's keys clinked quietly.

The woman standing in the doorway of the airplane was backlit. Hazel squinted at her.

"Hurry, Hazel!" the woman shouted over the buzz of the engines.

Hazel trotted up the steps. She grinned when the she reached the top and the woman's face was revealed. "Adele!"

They hugged briefly, then Adele stepped aside, ushering Hazel into the plane. "You're officially back in Canada now, Hazel."

"I suppose there are benefits to diplomacy." Hazel dropped her messenger bag on a seat. "Adele, I triggered all the disruptors before I left."

Adele laughed. "Fantastic. They were suspicious of you, Hazel, so they might check those weapons, but a couple of hours certainly won't hurt our cause."

"It's a shame that we can't just steal the pits. We could do so much with the fuel. That new reactor that's in development, or maybe some more medical isotopes for Sylvia—"

"Sylvia Fedoruk has plenty of fuel for her medical research," Adele said. "Anyway, I've got to get you back to Chalk River. The subs need some modification."

Hazel settled into her seat as Adele talked about the nuclear reactor in the submarine. Working on the reactor would be a nice break, but she was sure that she'd be reassigned soon as a nuclear disarmament Peacekeeper. Canada had been able to accomplish so much by harvesting moonshine. And they could do so much more.

IRONCLAD

Originally published in *Kisses by Clockwork*, edited by Liz Grzyb. Ticonderoga Publications, 2014.

I have a fondness for steampunk fiction—it's a wonderful way to combine heists and clockwork gadgets with my interest in history. As may be obvious from the anthology title, "Ironclad" also contains a romantic element.

IRONCLAD

Northern California, 1872

essica peered out the stagecoach door, ignoring the driver's
proffered, sweaty, hand. She wished, not for the first time,
that her boss had sprung for the expense of a steamcoach,
with all the luxuries that came with it, like clockwork drivers and
footmen. But in the aftermath of the War of the Southern
Rebellion, federal troops had come to the state to combat the
Indians, and clients were few. The profits from this small job
would stretch even further if costs were kept to a minimum.
Understanding the need for economy, however, did not soothe
her tender posterior.

She stepped off the stagecoach, one crimson boot skimming
over a steaming pile of horse dung before landing safely on the
warped wooden planks masquerading as a sidewalk. She released
her death grip on her skirt, allowing the rich fabric to swirl
around her ankles, kissing the ground and sending up a cloud of
dust. Peeling off her gloves, she examined the hotel in front of
her.

When the driver dropped her trunk beside her, Jessica laid a
hand on his arm. "I'll need assistance to my lodgings."

The man squinted at her. "This here is the only hotel in town."

Jessica pushed a stray lock of raven black hair behind her ear,
and smiled. "I believe there are rooms above The Painted Lady?"

"Yeah, but that's the—" The driver stopped talking and his

mouth hung slack for an instant. "Oh."

"I'll pay you for your time, of course." Not waiting for his stammering acceptance, Jessica strode towards the brothel, a pastel pink building that would have seemed sweet and innocent on the Bay, but in this dusty town, where white was a bold colour, it was shocking and rude.

The swinging doors were a cheerful lavender, and smooth beneath Jessica's touch as she pushed on them. She waited a few minutes in the entryway, allowing her eyes to adjust to the dim interior.

At the sound of her name, Jessica turned. A tall woman came out from behind the bar, laying a towel on the counter.

"Jessica?" the woman repeated. "I'm Eliza. I thought your coach was arriving later! I would have met you at the stop."

"We made good time. There wasn't any rain to slow us down." Jessica clasped Eliza's hands and kissed her on both cheeks, European fashion. "The driver has brought my trunk."

"Of course." Eliza glanced over Jessica's shoulder. "Up the stairs, last door on the right."

Jessica arched her back, discreetly working the kinks out. She was exhausted, but she had a job to do. "Daisy has left?"

"Yesterday. Her mother has taken ill." Eliza clucked, eyes twinkling. "Rather worrisome, sudden illnesses like that."

"Yes." Jessica forced a chuckle, although she didn't find the sudden illnesses of mothers to be the least bit amusing. "How fortunate that I was available to come and help you out. I understand Daisy has important patrons."

Eliza looked toward the stairs. "Ah, there is your driver. I'll show you to your room."

When the stagecoach driver had left, Eliza cupped Jessica's elbow and guided her to the stairs. "Now, you mustn't worry if you only entertain one person tonight, Jessica. The Painted Lady has been well compensated in anticipation of such an event."

Jessica sighed, one hand rubbing her hip, thinking of the jouncing coach ride. Apparently, the economy of the company did not extend to bribes.

The banister was dust-free; a royal purple carpet lined the stairs. The Painted Lady, Jessica thought, must entertain a lot to afford its upkeep. A row of doors lined the upper hallway, gaslight lanterns dotting the walls. Due to years of training and experience, she perused the hallway for any potential threats. Was that a person's shadow at the end of the hallway? A saloon girl? Or someone else?

She thought she heard the rasp of a wooden door rubbing against carpet. A curious girl then. Perfectly natural. There was no reason for Jessica to believe that anybody suspected her true reason for being at the brothel.

She willed her heartbeat to slow and kept her voice calm. "I'm relieved to hear that your establishment won't suffer financially, Eliza."

Eliza shot her a fleeting glance. "Daisy is one of our more popular girls. She's quite busy. Ah, here we are. You're right next door to Otto, so it should be fairly quiet for you and your guest. Guests."

"Otto?"

Eliza smiled, dimples appearing in her cheeks. "I'll introduce you."

The door next to Jessica's room stood open. Eliza stopped and rapped on it. "Otto?"

"Good afternoon, Miss Eliza." A tall, broad figure filled the doorway.

Jessica's eyes widened. A clockwork man! His joints moved with the characteristic jerkiness of his kind, but silently, indicating well-oiled gears and springs. Jessica calculated the expense of the oil needed to maintain the clockwork man in a town where dirt, grime, and dust were so pervasive, and whistled in appreciation. Her father would have given his eyeteeth to examine such a specimen as Otto.

Otto turned to her. His glass eyes looked real, as did the thatch of dark hair on his head. "Good day, Miss Jessica. I hear that we are to be neighbours."

"Yes," Jessica smiled. He was handsome by any standard, mechanical or organic. "I just arrived."

"Otto entertains our female guests," Eliza said. "I know it looks exorbitant, but we actually lost money when we had male hosts on staff." She lowered her voice. "Otto has better stamina."

"Oh." Jessica stifled a giggle and held out a hand. "Nice to meet you, Otto."

"The pleasure is all mine, Miss Jessica." The clockwork man took her hand. His skin was hairless, perfectly smooth, and the colour of aged ivory. It was the best replicant-skin that Jessica had ever seen; most of the clockwork men she knew had smooth metal plates covering their gears. "My evenings are seldom full." His thumb stroked the sensitive skin on her inner wrist, and to her annoyance, Jessica felt a wave of heat roll over her body.

She extracted her hand from his grasp. "You must excuse me, I have to freshen up after the long coach ride. I'll see you later, Otto."

He bowed his head and retreated into his room.

Eliza laughed and opened Jessica's door, handing the key to Jessica. "He's a marvel, isn't he? The latest in clockwork men. A wonderful gadget."

Jessica managed a smile. "Thanks, Eliza. When should I come down?"

"We start entertaining at seven." Eliza nodded. "Have a pleasant afternoon, Jessica. You may want to take a nap."

Jessica shut the door and leaned against it, waiting for her body to cool. Now was not the time to get flustered by a little male attention, especially the attention of an artificial man. Never mind that Otto was the most sophisticated clockwork man she'd ever seen . . . and being her father's daughter, she knew good clockwork.

A servant rapped at the door, bearing a tray laden with dishes. Jessica lifted the lid of one, revealing several dainty cucumber sandwiches—cucumber! Her mind boggled at the expense of shipping that by steamcoach. The Painted Lady operated as if having federal troops stationed in California hadn't driven up the price of, well, *everything*.

Once she had devoured half a dozen of the tiny sandwiches, Jessica was able to concentrate on the task at hand. She would have, at most, two nights to accomplish this job. She could only envision it taking that long if her mark did not appear this evening.

After peering out into the hallway, Jessica locked her door and opened her trunk. She pawed through dresses, underclothes, lingerie, and nightdresses, tossing them haphazardly aside, caring little if they landed on the floor or the bed. A modest jewellery box rested on the bottom of the trunk. She set that on the floor, leaving the trunk bare. Jessica hooked her fingers around the edges of a knot that marred the golden plank, and heaved. Within a couple of minutes, she had worked the board free, revealing the space beneath the false bottom.

Jessica took out the hand cannon first, loaded it, and tucked it beneath the plump feather pillow on her bed. Next came the medical equipment: the syringe, vials, and stethoscope. The top drawer of the bedside table would do for now; she knew many soiled doves who had similar paraphernalia in their rooms. Her gold pocket watch, which contained a tiny photographic camera within its geared innards, also came out. Spyglass, badge, and portable steam-powered telegraph remained in the trunk. If she needed those, it would be because the job had gone to hell. And that shouldn't happen—how difficult could it be to seduce a scientist?

The last item removed was a thin, plain envelope, the colour of bone, with a scarlet wax seal. After a moment's hesitation, Jessica also placed this in the top drawer of the bedside table. Then she replaced the false bottom and pushed the trunk over to the armoire.

She placed her small jewellery box on the top shelf of the armoire. Cunning tools and gadgets were concealed in her necklaces, rings, and bracelets, even her earrings. Wonderful accessories that people expected to see on a woman, needing no explanation for their presence. Next, she hung up her clothes.

With the aid of a button hook, Jessica removed her boots. The heel of the right boot popped off into her hand with a gentle twist; she removed a piece of paper that had been folded into a square. She clutched the paper for a moment, unease fluttering in her stomach. Being found with this particular piece of paper could ruin her life.

Shaking her head, Jessica grabbed another pair of boots, the ones she intended to wear that night. She didn't have anything to worry about. Her mother had died so long ago that Jessica was the only one left who had known her. It would take quite a detective to uncover her origins. The job hadn't been compromised.

She sprung open one of the heels and inserted the paper into it. Closing the heel, she set the new pair of boots onto the floor of the armoire.

And then, finally, Jessica collapsed onto the bed.

Humming, she reached down the front of her dress, wriggled her fingers into her corset, and dredged out a battered photograph. Jessica studied the image. A man, aged about thirty, wearing goggles and a laboratory coat, stared out of the grainy image. She'd been examining the photograph for a few days now, since her boss had assigned her this job. She thought she'd recognize him in person.

She put the photograph into the bedside table, curled up against the pillow—fingertips brushing the hand cannon—and shut her eyes.

Promptly at seven she descended the stairs, dressed in a sapphire blue gown with a modest neckline and a very long train. The sleeves were tight from her wrist to elbow, and slightly puffed from her elbow to shoulder. It was the height of fashion and very respectable, all the way down to the front hem . . . which ended at her upper thighs. Her stockings and garters were sheer white, her boots a blue to match the dress. Jessica's black hair was caught loosely at the nape of her neck, with a few tendrils curling about her cheeks. Her only adornments were a golden locket and a sapphire ring.

Many eyes followed her progress down the stairs, but not the ones she wanted to see.

After spending ninety minutes flirting with the men, Jessica had a better idea of how The Painted Lady could afford its upkeep. Soldiers. Officers. She sipped from yet another cup of tea, studying them from the corners of her eyes. The presence of a military fort in the town had not been in her dossier for this assignment . . . yet it did make sense, considering the occupation of her mark. And the men who weren't officers or soldiers, who were they? Not farmers, she judged, eyeing their well-cut clothes. More scientists? But that didn't add up. She'd been near most of the men at one point or another, between singing, dancing, and socializing, and those suited men didn't smell of coal, oil, or chemicals.

The lavender doors swung open.

Jessica's eyes flew to it, as they had all evening, and a soft sigh of relief spilled from her lips when she saw it was him. Taller than she'd expected, and better-looking than the picture she had—of course, the picture wasn't a full body shot, and he wore goggles in it—but it was definitely him. The puzzle of The Painted Lady's patrons would have to wait.

Jessica rose from the arm of the chair and drifted over to him; he had not ventured far into the room. "Dr. Brown?"

Startled blue eyes flicked to her. "Good evening." His gaze swept down her body and back up, lingering at a few spots. "I don't believe we've met."

"I'm Jessica. May I pour you a drink, Dr. Brown?"

The scientist frowned. "No need for such formality. I go by Wes here."

"Certainly, Wes. Now, what I can I get you?"

"Oh . . ." Wes turned his head, looking over and around her. "I usually keep time with Daisy."

Jessica *tsk*ed. "Daisy's mother took ill, and Daisy has left to nurse her." Daisy's mother's illness had cleared up immediately upon receipt of the steamcoach tickets to the Bay, where reservations at The Palace Hotel awaited them. The client had wanted to ensure that Daisy would not be tempted to renege on the agreement. It was a pity that her boss hadn't negotiated a larger fee, Jessica mused, since the client had to be loaded. Her posterior would certainly have appreciated it.

Wes blinked. "In that case, I should be delighted to have a drink with you, Jessica."

Jessica beamed up at him and curled an arm around his elbow. She wrinkled her nose at the faint odor of coal that hung about him. He must have come straight from his lab.

She deposited him into a chair, then strolled to the bar. Otto had replaced the bartender.

"I see you have met Wes," Otto said. "It must have been hard to wait this long for him."

"What do you mean? I'm here to entertain gentlemen." Jessica snapped her fingers. "I forgot to ask what he wanted to drink."

"Our dear doctor always orders the same drink. I have no difficulty recalling his preference." The clockwork man pulled a glass tumbler from the shelf and held it beneath the counter where the kegs were stored. "You remarked earlier on Daisy's important patrons, yet have ignored several of them. When Wes entered, you immediately went to his side, something you have not done all evening."

Jessica's eyelids drifted to half-mast, and she regarded the clockwork man through her lashes. She was sure the other women had noticed her behaviour—it was their job, after all. But for Otto to notice . . . Had the clockwork man overheard her conversation with Eliza that afternoon? And, more importantly, how much had he inferred from that conversation? She forced a trilling laugh. "What an active imagination you have, Otto!"

The clockwork man blinked at her, looking puzzled, if a mechanical construct could be said to have emotion. His eyes flickered, and his expression lightened. He leaned across the bar. "I understand," he said in a low voice that sent shivers running up her spine. "I risk your cover by saying so much."

The smell of oil filled her nose, sparking happy memories of her father's machine shop. Forcing aside the pleasurable feelings Otto aroused in her, Jessica said coldly, "I don't know what you're talking about."

Otto nodded. "Of course."

Avoiding his gaze, she concentrated on his movements as he filled the tumbler, enjoying the slight jerks that marred the otherwise steady motions. Reluctant admiration for Otto's reasoning skills filled her—there weren't many people, men or women, who could out-think her—but they posed a risk to her right now. Her Leyden jar would have been ideal for the situation, for the electricity would wreak havoc on Otto's metal body and intricate gears, but she had not brought the bulky apparatus with her. She drummed her fingers on the bar. Perhaps the hand cannon? She shook her head. Ignoring him was the safest course—she doubted her boss could afford to replace him.

Otto handed the full glass to Jessica.

She sniffed. "Sarsaparilla?" She cursed under her breath. She'd been hoping for a little alcohol to grease the task ahead of her. She twisted the ring on her finger. Time for plan B.

"It is what he drinks," Otto said. He cocked his head at her. "Would you like an iced beverage? Your cheeks are flushed."

"I'm fine, thank you, Otto." Jessica clutched the drink to her chest. "I should return to Wes, before one of the other girls poaches him."

The clockwork man nodded. He leaned over the bar again. "I am sure you will be more comfortable away from the soldiers, given the circumstances."

"Circumstances?"

"The war that they wage against your people."

Jessica's mind blanked for an instant. With effort, she focused on her facial muscles, quirking an eyebrow. "Otto, nobody is waging war on my 'people'." She injected concern into her voice. "Have you had a diagnostic recently?"

Otto frowned. "I apologize. Your hair . . . eyes . . . facial structure . . . I assumed . . . ."

Jessica smiled weakly. She did not need a bored clockwork man taking such an interest in her. No one involved with this job would appreciate the attention. "Why, Otto, are you *flirting* with me? And while I'm working too. Shame!" She playfully slapped his wrist.

Otto's eyes swirled. "Ah. Discretion."

Jessica saluted him with the glass. "Thanks for the drink."

She knew that he watched her leave. When she had settled on the arm of Wes's chair, she glanced over her shoulder at the bar. Otto had propped his elbows on the dark mahogany surface and was staring at her.

"The clockwork man is amazing," Wes said. He sipped at the drink and peered around her to the bar. "I'd love to examine him up close. He's a sophisticated machine."

"Would it prove useful for your research?" Jessica asked. She ran her fingers through Wes's hair, massaging his temples.

"Maybe." He grabbed her hand. "No more talk about work. Let's go upstairs."

Keeping her hand gripped in his own, Wes stood, drawing Jessica to her feet. Clasped hands held high, as if they were stepping onto the dance floor, they went upstairs. Jessica led Wes down the hall to her room and waved him inside. As she closed the door, a single, dark shape appeared at the top of the stairs. She scowled.

Jessica arranged a smile on her face as she turned back to Wes. He wasted no time. Wrapping his arm, still holding her hand, around her back, he pulled her to his chest and kissed her.

He was a good kisser, Jessica thought in surprise, especially for someone who spent so much time in the lab that his only female companions were those he paid for. However . . . there was work to be done. She pulled away. "Another drink, Wes? Something . . . hot, perhaps?"

Wes regarded her from half-closed eyes. "In this heat?"

A more genuine smile spread over her face. "Do you know that drinking a warm beverage on a warm day helps cool you more than a cold one?"

"Hmmm . . . yes, I see how that might work. Fix some tea then, and we'll test your assertion."

On the chest of drawers next to the washing pitcher and bowl, there was a copper and glass steam kettle. It wasn't pretty, but she supposed attractiveness had been sacrificed for the sake of convenience. Jessica had seen one in a judge's office once but had never operated one. She measured tea leaves into the kettle, poured water from the pitcher, and, moving with a sureness that she didn't feel, used the flint striker to ignite the boiler.

"Is that safe?" Wes asked.

"Perfectly," Jessica said, hoping it was true. She turned back to him. "That will take a few minutes to come to a boil. Where were we?"

Wes smiled. "You were in the process of losing your clothes."

Jessica arched a brow. "I don't remember that. But you're correct, it is a trifle warm in here." A true lady's garment would have had a million tiny buttons down the back: impossible to undo without help. Jessica had borrowed this dress from a saloon girl. All the buttons were down the front.

She wasn't sure how to be seductive about taking off a dress, so Jessica undid them matter-of-factly, keeping her eyes on Wes. He seemed to like it, his cheeks flushing. With a final flick of her fingers, Jessica worked the last button open, pulled her arms from the tight sleeves, and let the dress fall to the floor.

Other than being chillier, standing there in her corset, pantalettes, and stockings didn't feel much different from her usual work clothes. It certainly wasn't as shocking as her men's trousers and vests. The hoity-toity types in San Francisco would probably prefer her in her undergarments—at least they were feminine.

The tea kettle shrieked.

Grabbing the thick towel that lay on the chest, Jessica picked up the kettle and poured tea into the delicate china cups. "Sugar, Wes?"

At his affirmative, she added two lumps. At the same time, her pinky finger deftly flipped open her sapphire ring. A slight jiggle of her finger sent a trickle of powder into the cup. She stirred, closing the ring with another flick of her pinky.

Jessica carried the two cups back to the bed where Wes sat propped against the brass headboard. She handed him the doctored cup, took a sip from her own. "And now for the experiment."

Wes nodded, taking a hearty gulp from his own cup. He lowered it and blinked at her. His pupils were dilated, the blue iris almost entirely swallowed by black. "I feel . . . strange." His eyes drifted shut and his head lolled against the headboard.

Jessica kissed his cheek. "I do apologize, but I need something from you." She turned from him, opening the top drawer of the nightstand. The opiate he had ingested would ease the use of the serum she would inject into his bloodstream.

Her hands were caught in a vise-like grip. "Really? And what would that be?"

Jessica's head whipped around. Wes's pupils were still dilated, but only just. The opiate was wearing off. "But—you can't!"

"I take pills to combat such tactics. I'm not stupid, and neither are my investors." His eyes were shrewd. "Who do you represent?"

Jessica tugged. He tightened his grasp, and she had to clench her jaw to keep from gasping again, this time in pain. "I don't know who the client is," she said, "but I am a Pinkerton operative."

"Pinkerton? Pinkerton hires . . . ?" His eyes swept over her half-naked body and his lip curled with disdain.

Jessica straightened, bringing her knee up into his groin. Wes gasped. He let go of her as his hands moved down to the offended area, and Jessica dove around him, shoved a hand under the pillow, and grabbed her hand cannon. She rolled off the bed, twisted, and landed facing Wes, hand cannon pointed at him. His hands were still cupped protectively over his groin, but his blue eyes watched her.

"Pinkerton doesn't, in fact, hire—" She pointed her finger to the floor, where the faint sounds of the piano and laughing men and women drifted through the boards. "I was willing to play nice to get the blueprints, but since the drugs won't work, we'll do this the hard way."

Someone knocked on the door. Jessica didn't take her eyes from Wes. "Who is it?" she asked, making her voice as throaty as possible. "I'm a little busy at the moment."

"It is Otto. I was wondering if I could be of assistance?"

Wes opened his mouth and Jessica rammed the muzzle of her hand cannon against his cheek. "Shhh." Relief swept over her. With Otto's logic gears and strength . . . Hell and damnation, what was she thinking? Raising her voice, she said, "No, thank you, Otto. We're just fine here."

After a moment of silence, Otto said, "I have excellent hearing, Jessica. I am offering to help you with your . . . work."

Her seduce-and-drug-the-scientist plan was unravelling before her eyes. Her boss would have a fit if she brought a civilian, even an artificial one, onto the case. Unless . . . Jessica narrowed her eyes and scrutinized Wes. His eyes were wide; his forehead beaded with sweat. Fear.

She sighed. So, the clockwork man and the scientist weren't playing an elaborate game with her. "Come in then, Otto."

The clockwork man entered, shutting the door behind him. Jessica tossed him the key, and he turned it in the lock, leaving it there.

The hand cannon was still directed at Wes, but Jessica made sure to keep the clockwork man in her field of vision. She was reasonably certain that he meant her no harm, but made of metal, powered by gears and springs, he was a lot stronger than her. If he wanted to cause trouble . . . well, her increasingly not-so-simple job would get interesting in a hurry.

"How do you think you can help me, Otto?"

He ignored the question. "Is it true you are a Pinkerton operative?"

Otto's voice was childlike in its excitement. Jessica's lips twitched. A fanatic. The knot in her stomach loosened. "Yes. I have my badge, but for obvious reasons I can't show it to you at the moment."

Otto nodded. "I have always wondered if perhaps my skills are wasted in my current occupation. If I help you, do you think you could provide a letter of recommendation to your employer? I enjoy investigating."

Which explained his lurking about in hallways and eavesdropping. "Yes. *If* my mission is successful." A clockwork operative! Jessica smiled, imagining the hefty bonus for recruiting an agent of Otto's strength and abilities. *And* she would have an opportunity to see him again. "Your plan is . . . ?"

"There is a saying that you catch more flies with honey than vinegar."

"I like honey," Wes said.

Jessica's eyes didn't waver from the scientist. Her wrist ached. "What if honey doesn't work?"

"I am strong enough to break bones," Otto said. Something whirred and Jessica risked a quick peek. Otto's pupils were contracting, focusing on her arm. "He hurt you. I see the bruising."

Telescopic lenses? Jessica wondered. She'd have to ask him later. Maybe while she was at it, she'd ask him how he could sound angry, as if he had emotions.

"I said that I like honey!"

Jessica took a deep breath. "Thank you, Otto, for reminding me of my options. I do have some honey." She lowered her hand cannon. "But first, Wes, I need to ascertain that you have the information I was hired to find. Your research—are you developing a steam-powered, armoured tractor?"

Wes pinched the bridge of his nose. After a few moments of silence, he looked up at her, resigned. "What do you want?"

And here it was. Jessica picked up her long-forgotten tea cup and gulped the contents, grimacing at the tepid liquid. She put the empty cup back down on the bedside table. "I have a job offer, in writing." Jessica opened the drawer of the bedside table and removed the ivory envelope with the unadorned scarlet seal. "From the organization that engaged Pinkerton. They will accept copies of the plans in lieu of employment. And they also demand the name of your investor."

Wes stretched out a hand for the envelope, but Jessica held it out of his reach. "I also have this . . ." She leaned down and grabbed the heel of her right boot. With a sharp twist, the heel swung open and the compact, folded square of paper plopped to the floor. Jessica scooped up the paper, snapped the heel back into place, and straightened. "Another offer from a third party," she said, handing both the envelope and the thick fold of paper to Wes.

"You're betraying Pinkerton?"

It shouldn't have hurt so much to disappoint a mechanical man. Jessica shook her head. "I've given the scientist his job offer; my task for Pinkerton will be completed when I relay his response to my boss. I'm simply providing Dr Brown with another . . . option."

Otto hummed, eye lenses whirring lazily, but made no other response.

Wes popped the seal of the envelope with a fingernail and scanned the contents. He read it again, more slowly. The corner of his mouth curled upwards and then he threw back his head and laughed. When the guffaws had tapered to chuckles, he tucked the letter back into the envelope, which he slid inside his shirt.

"An invitation to clown school?" Jessica asked, irked.

He shook his head and unfolded the thick square of paper. After reading it through twice, he refolded it with slow, precise movements and tucked it into his shirt with the envelope.

"Do you know who Pinkerton's client is?" Wes asked.

"I suspect," Jessica said, "that the client is Army Intelligence. They worked hard to keep the organization's identity a secret, but," she shrugged, "they're easy to spot once you know what to look for."

"And the other?"

Jessica's mouth pinched at the corners. She hated divulging her own secrets. "That's personal."

Wes nodded. "My investors are a new intelligence branch of the government, independent of the Army or Navy Intelligence offices. They call themselves the Secret Service."

The men in suits downstairs. Government agents. Her breath hissed out. Nothing could ever be simple.

"The colleagues of the Army officers are your investors?" Otto asked, coming to the same conclusion. "But why are they developing it here instead of the East coast? Would they not want these armoured tractors for use in case the unrest in Europe affects us?"

Jessica gave Otto a look of approval. She'd never interacted with a clockwork man so capable of thinking outside its programming. Hell, she knew a sad number of flesh and blood people who couldn't think their way out of a cardboard box. "Well, Wes?"

Wes squirmed, cheeks flushing. "The second letter confirms a rather uncomfortable hypothesis I've had for some time now."

He'd never come out and say it. "Otto, they're going to use the tractors—"

"Oh!" the clockwork man blurted. "The Indian campaigns." He paused, then repeated in a much softer voice, "Oh."

"I imagine an armoured tractor will be useful on the lava ridges," Jessica said.

Wes grunted. "If I can figure out the wheels. I need it to crawl, to gain traction, not roll . . ." He cleared his throat. "My apologies. Yes, I suspect my research will be used on our own soil first."

"Against the Indians," Jessica growled.

"As you say. Against the Indians," Wes said.

Otto placed a cool hand on her shoulder. "What have the Modoc offered you to desist with your research?"

Wes looked her straight in the eyes. "Not enough. Not enough for the repercussions I'd have to face."

Jessica sagged, relishing the chance to lean against Otto, who wouldn't bend, or wilt, or break. She hadn't thought that her mother's people would be able to come up with enough money to bribe the scientist—and what else could they offer? They had no land, no appreciable wealth.

Otto squeezed her shoulder. "How likely are the Modoc to initiate peace talks?"

Jessica sighed. "There have been talks, but they won't return to the Klamath reservation." She shrugged. "But I believe there will continue to be talks, as long as their fighting ability remains somewhat equal to that of the Army."

"I won't sabotage my own research!"

"Now, Doctor, nobody suggested anything of the sort," Otto soothed.

Yet, Jessica thought wryly. But what additional honey did Otto have to offer?

"I am the only one of my model," Otto said. "My inventor has patented his work, of course, so I cannot show you much, but a look at my arm servos and gears should prove illuminating to one interested in clockwork mechanisms."

The comforting presence of Otto's hand left her shoulder. Otto stepped closer to Wes, rolling up one pristine white sleeve. He grabbed his left wrist with his right hand, twisted, and removed the left hand from its arm, revealing dozens of tiny, interlocking gears, clicking and clacking as their teeth moved against each other, shiny cams, and springs.

Wes craned his head. He pursed his lips, a low whistle escaping. Jessica goggled at the exposed gears. Even with a tinker for a father, Otto's gearwork was beyond her comprehension. He was beautiful.

"What materials does he use?" Wes asked, leaning close to Otto's arm.

Otto cocked his head and hummed. "I cannot say. You may have a photograph."

Wes nodded, his fingers twitching. "I need a pen," he muttered. He pulled a jeweller's loupe from his pocket, held it up to his eye, and squinted at Otto's exposed gears. Sighing, he rested against the headboard, returned the loupe to his pocket, and crossed his arms over his chest. "With a gear system like that, I could . . . the patents . . . my research . . . The trade is acceptable."

Jessica relaxed her jaw as tension ebbed from her body. She thumbed open her locket.

"Trick jewellery?" Otto asked. His pupils dilated, whirring.

"Yes," she said. She pressed a button, and the innards of the locket expanded on a tiny accordion. "Hold out your arm, Otto."

Jessica held the locket up to her eye and peered at Otto's arm through the tiny lens. Making adjustments with the minuscule knobs, she brought Otto's arm into focus. Then, holding her breath, she depressed the clasp. The camera clicked. She took two more photographs, to ensure that at least one would be of sufficient quality and clarity for their purposes, then tapped another button to close the camera.

Shutting the locket, she turned to Wes. "I can develop those photographs tonight and have them for you tomorrow."

Otto harrumphed. "One."

Jessica nodded. "One," she repeated. "Thank you, Otto."

Wes slid out of the bed, adjusted his shirt and trousers. "Under the circumstances, I will refuse the employment offer of your client, and the demand for blueprints." He held out a hand.

Jessica clasped his hand. "I'm sure once the client is informed of your investor's identity, your refusal will be accepted." She hesitated. "And the other?"

"Thank them, certainly, but they needn't worry about paying me. Coincidentally," Wes said, winking, "my current research is floundering. It may be years before I can find my way to a solution."

Jessica closed her eyes briefly, concealing the surge of emotion that overcame her. "That's certainly tragic," Jessica said. "Be sure to talk with Eliza on your next visit to The Painted Lady. I'm sure she can cheer you up."

Wes raised her hand, brushing his lips across her knuckles. Releasing her hand, he turned to the clockwork man. "Otto, a privilege to meet you."

The two shook hands. "I hope your clockwork research is successful, Dr. Brown," Otto said.

When the sound of Wes's footfalls on the stairs had faded, Otto cocked his head at Jessica. "So, partner, when do we head back to the office?"

Jessica's pulse pounded in her neck. The smell of oil surrounded her, and she could just hear the gentle clicks of his gears. "Only business partners?"

Otto's eyes dilated, and Jessica detected a hitch in his clicking. "But I am not human. Miss Eliza says I'm amusing, but I am only a tool. I can't be a companion."

"You're the only being I've met that's smart enough to keep up with me. And you—you are kind. And steadfast. I don't care what these people think." Jessica smiled. "To answer your question, we don't have to leave until tomorrow, after I give Eliza Wes's photograph for safekeeping."

Otto cupped her elbows with his cold hands. "I find the idea of being more than business partners . . . pleasing."

With a husky laugh, Jessica grabbed a fistful of Otto's shirt and pulled his head down for a kiss.

MADAM LIBRARIAN

Originally published in *Hear Me Roar,* edited by Rhonda Parrish. Poise and Pen Publishing, 2020.

Fun fact! I worked in academic libraries for over a decade. I fully admit that I'm stretching sci-fi and all things "punk" a lot with the inclusion of this story, but I like it so much that I've decided bookbinding makes this library-punk. (Yes, I made that up—but wouldn't that be a fun, themed anthology?)

MADAM LIBRARIAN

Miriam smiled as she took the neon-coloured board book from the toddler, ignoring the sticky patches on the cover. The child's mother bleated a nervous apology.

"Nothing a little soap won't fix," Miriam assured her, and the mother's face relaxed as she tugged her child towards the library's main entrance.

Miriam chuckled as she followed them. Maybe she'd tell the next nervous parent that jam didn't bother her at all—not like the acrid odor of the potty-training books. She wore rubber gloves handling those, until they'd been disinfected.

She waved to the child as she locked the entrance. There. Another day at the Erebville Library completed. Her smile faded as she turned away from the door. Time for the library board meeting. The first item on tonight's agenda was a challenge to one of the Young Adult novels in the collection, *Flowers' Waltz* by Delia Strike. The board director, Kenneth, wanted the book removed, and Miriam was anticipating a heated discussion.

Miriam sniffed. She hadn't banned a book in all her years as librarian.

She paused at the kitchenette tucked into one corner of the staff workroom, and her mouth puckered with annoyance. None of the board members had bothered to put on the kettle when they'd brewed coffee. Mindful that she was now tardy, Miriam poured a cup of coffee and stirred several sugars into it. The bitter odor irritated her nostrils, despite the added sugar.

No one looked up at her as she entered the meeting room. Amy, her long-time friend and president of the Library Friends fundraising group, shuffled papers and stared at the table. Petra, the student member of the board, was focused on her phone, her face blank and stony. Miriam's gaze swept the table, but everyone avoided her glare . . . except Kenneth, who smirked at her, his small, piggy eyes gleaming.

"So glad you could *finally* join us, Miriam," he said. "We were just about to vote on our first agenda item."

"Vote?" she repeated. The library board rarely surprised her, but now she was stunned. Her eyes flicked to the clock. "I'm only three minutes late, and you're voting on *Flowers' Waltz* already?"

Kenneth shrugged. "It's not a difficult debate, Miriam. We can't have filth like this"—he pointed to the glitter bedecked book on the table—"in our library."

"*My* library," she said sharply.

"*Our* library," he said again. "The board's library. You're just an employee."

Miriam took a hasty gulp of coffee. The scalding drink seared its way down her gullet, burning away any rash words she might have spat at Kenneth. After all, silence nourished wisdom, according to Francis Bacon.

At least the horrid drink was good for something, she thought as she stalked to her seat by Amy. Her friend, as usual, smelled faintly of dried grass, which always reminded Miriam of her youth, and the sheep in the nearby meadow.

"Very well," Miriam said, calmly, "as your employee, I'd like to point out that *Flowers' Waltz* depicts loving, healthy relationships between teenagers, providing reassura—"

"We've already discussed the book," Kenneth interrupted. "It's time to vote. All in favour of removing *Flowers' Waltz* from our shelves?"

Miriam kept her hands flat on the table. Amy did likewise.

"Petra?" prompted Kenneth impatiently.

The teenager set down her phone. "Miss Thorn, isn't there anything you can do?" she asked, looking at Miriam directly. "They decided about the book before they even got here."

"Miss Thorn can't do anything. She was late, and it's now time to vote," Kenneth said sternly. "How are you voting, Petra?"

"Nay," she said, stuffing her hands in her pockets.

The resolution passed five to three. All eyes flew to Miriam as Kenneth announced the outcome for the minutes, but Miriam didn't crumple under their stares. She raised her coffee cup, obscuring her face, and forced down another swallow of the bitter drink.

An anger like nothing she'd felt in decades burned in her belly. The nerve of these people, making decisions about *her* books.

She felt her cheeks tighten and her smile become more brittle as the meeting progressed. Amy passed her a miniature chocolate bar, murmuring about blood sugar.

Miriam popped the entire sweet into her mouth, hoping the chocolate would dampen her anger. She needed to get a hold of herself, or else there'd be another Incident. Nobody on this board was old enough to remember, but Miriam had found the process of building a new library stressful and exhausting. She couldn't do that again.

The painful memories doused her anger, and she was able to finish the meeting without biting anyone's head off.

"Can I give you a ride home, Miriam?" Amy asked as they meandered with the other board members to the staff entrance.

"I still have to close up the library, but thank you, Amy." Miriam leaned closer to her friend and whispered, "The chocolate worked wonders."

Amy smiled and patted her purse. "I never leave home without a stash."

"Quite sensible of you, my dear," Miriam said. They hugged, and Amy ambled out to her car.

A few more board members left, and Miriam managed to politely bid them farewell. Soon it was Petra's turn through the exit.

"I thought you'd be able to do something," Petra said as she pulled on a denim jacket.

"I am sorry, Petra," Miriam said. "Kenneth outmanoeuvred me this time. I'll put together a counter-proposal for the next meeting."

"Really?" Petra asked.

Miriam nodded. "Really."

Some of the stoniness melted from the girl's face, and she smiled. "Thanks, Miss Thorn."

And with her departure, Kenneth was the last board member left. Miriam held the door for him.

"Petra sure has a lot of confidence in you," he said.

"I *am* the librarian," she said, brows arching.

He nodded. "Yeah, but there's something more, isn't there, Miriam? You're not just a librarian."

Her face froze; she could feel the muscles stiffening. "I don't know what you're talking about, Kenneth," she said softly. "I've been the Erebville librarian since before you were born." She pulled the door open another few inches. "Now, I have to finish closing the building for the night."

Kenneth stepped forward, but paused in the doorway. "This isn't over, Miriam. That filthy book doesn't belong on our shelves, so don't try any tricks."

Then he faded into the darkness of the parking lot, and she was alone, finally.

She proceeded with her usual closing tasks: shutting down the computers and copier machine, emptying the recycling bins, straightening the circulation desk. She wiped clean the jam-splotched book the toddler had enjoyed so much. Then she trudged to the meeting room.

There were half a dozen copies of *Flowers' Waltz*—it was insanely popular with the teenaged girls. And, she knew, the tween girls as well, although she'd kept that tidbit of information from the library board. The official reason for removing the book was its depiction of lesbian relationships. But what she suspected really stuck in their craw was that the book showed girls and women having full and happy lives without men.

It was an important book, especially in a small, stodgy town like Erebville, where gender roles were rigid.

Sighing, Miriam gathered up the books and carried them to her desk. With the automated system, it took just a couple of minutes to have the books formally withdrawn from the collection. She didn't stamp them, though. She stared thoughtfully into space for several minutes, and then she shut down her computer.

Tucking the books under her arm, she turned off the lights to the library. The dark didn't bother her, and she easily made her way to the supply closet. Her fingers hooked the latch under the shelf struts, and the rear wall opened with a click.

A dim, orange glow illuminated a staircase. Miriam trotted down the familiar, narrow stairs. At the bottom, she inhaled deeply, with pleasure. She loved the smell of books. She especially loved the smell of books in her true workspace.

Books were everywhere. On the bookcases that lined the walls. Stacked haphazardly on the floor. In piles on her large, wooden desk. They covered every available surface, except for a narrow path that weaved from the stairs to a large circular patch directly in front of her desk. In the low light provided by strategically placed floor lamps, the books shone warmly. Miriam adored all the books in her library, but these—these were special. These were *hers*.

Over the years, books had to be withdrawn from the collection. Broken; missing pages; old editions. She brought them all down here, to her workspace, where they were given new bindings, pages were repaired or replaced, and they were read and loved. While her library had several book repair tools, it was this space, her lair, that had specialized equipment for extensive repairs and preservation.

She cleared a space on her desk, pushing aside an inkwell and quill, her old-fashioned nameplate, and a shrivelled apple. She set the short stack of books down and drummed her fingers on the desk, thinking. Finally, she nodded. Not only had she promised Petra, but *Flowers' Waltz* was important. *Knowledge* was important.

Miriam extended her right pointer finger at the books. The finger elongated, her skin peeling to reveal copper scales, her nail splitting to release a long, sickle-shaped claw.

She opened the first book and, using her claw, sliced along the crease of the inner hinges, separating the manuscript—the text block—from the front and back covers. From there, it was relatively simple to separate the text block from the spine. She tossed the used cover to the floor and repeated the process on the next book.

When she had six sets of bound text blocks, Miriam knelt on the floor to rummage through a trunk that abutted her desk.

What sort of material to cover the books? Buckram, perhaps? Yes . . . a wonderfully dull, tan buckram. It would repel adults' gazes, dismissed as stuffy literature. Old books.

It took some time, even for someone as skilled as she, to measure and cut the boards and buckram to fit her text blocks. Fortunately, Miriam didn't need much sleep.

She had just decided on a new title—*Botany: Wild Roses*—and was preparing her stamping machine to emboss the covers, when she heard footsteps.

Her breath caught. Someone dared to enter her sanctuary? Scowling, her belly broiling with anger again, she set down the new cover and called, "Hello?"

The footsteps paused, then clattered down the stairs. It was Kenneth. His eyes were wide and his cheeks flushed.

Miriam stood up. "What are you doing here?"

"What is this place?" He gawked at the towers of books. "This isn't in the library blueprints!"

"This is my workshop," she growled. "What are you doing here?"

"I wanted to talk about that filthy book," Kenneth said. "But you weren't home. So, I came back here." He took a few steps toward her, parting his lips in an oily smile. "You see, I know your secret."

Miriam kept very still, not daring to even twitch. This again. She'd been careful—not toasting her own marshmallows during breaks at work and taking only the occasional flights during nights of the new moon. No, she reasoned, he didn't know about her true self. She relaxed, tilting her head. "Oh?"

"Yeah." He stepped closer. "I know that you're really Delia Strike, the author of *Flowers' Waltz*! That's why Petra thought you could keep it in circulation!"

Miriam laughed. She howled, bent over and clutching her stomach, as the laughter bubbled out of her. When it subsided, she straightened, wiping a tear from the corner of her eye. "Oh, I needed that. Thank you, Kenneth."

Kenneth blinked. "I don't understand."

"Of course not." Miriam gave him one of the patient smiles she used on unruly children. "I'm not secretly an author, Kenneth. I don't know where you got such an outlandish idea. But we do need to talk about you finding my lair."

"Your—what?" He shuffled closer and peered at the nameplate

on her desk. "Your name is spelled wrong."

"Is it?" Miriam spun it around.

WYRM, it read.

Miriam turned it to face Kenneth again. "I think my current name is a clever take on it, don't you? I'll miss it. I'll have to create a new one when 'Miriam' retires."

Kenneth was starting to look less confused and more afraid. She liked that look on him.

She stepped around the desk. "You silly human. I've been librarian of Erebville since 1754. First, you try to take my treasure, and now you've defiled my lair. What *am* I going to do with you?"

She grinned, showing off too-large and too many teeth. Kenneth squealed and stumbled backwards, landing on his rump. The pungent odor of urine bit the air. One of the book towers teetered and fell, scattering books.

"Don't eat me!" he cried.

"Eat you?" Miriam laughed again, smoke curling from her mouth. "Oh no, I'm not going to eat you. Humans taste terrible."

Her nose and jaw stretched into something resembling a crocodile's snout. A jet of flame streamed from her maw.

"However, I can't let you live, either," she said, leaning forward to inspect the pile of ash on her floor. She sighed, more smoke seeping from her mouth. She had important book binding to do, and now she had to cover up Kenneth's late-night visit as well.

Worst case scenario, there would be a repeat of the Incident of 1902, when she'd burned the library to the ground. That had been traumatic, for both her and the town, and she didn't think it would come to that. The library didn't have any alarmed doors or security cameras, thanks to Kenneth's penny-pinching ways, so all she had to do was return his car to his home, maybe start a little rumour about Kenneth's out-of-state girlfriend at the Seniors' Tea tomorrow, and let the police investigation run its course.

Humming, she turned to her desk and stroked the pile of buckram-covered boards and text blocks. "Soon you'll be on the shelves," she crooned. A few quiet recommendations would see *Botany: Wild Roses* in the hands of every girl in town. She'd personally give a copy to Petra.

Bacon seemed appropriate again. "*Ipsa scientia potestas est,*" she murmured as she swept the ashes into a tidy pile. "Knowledge is power, Kenneth, and my humans will be properly equipped."

Ribbons of smoke trickled from her maw as she chuckled, disposing of the ashes.

OF BIRDS AND BLOOD

Originally published Rhonda Parrish's newsletter, 2018.

I submitted this story for a dieselpunk fairy tale anthology and was terribly disappointed when it was rejected. However, the editor, Rhonda Parrish, wanted to use the story for promotional purposes, so the story didn't languish for long. "Of Birds and Blood" is a riff on the Grimms' fairy tale "Fitcher's Bird", a story that belongs in the Bluebeard family of tales. Please take that as a content warning: Bluebeard murdered his wives in horrible ways, and this story is gorier than most of my stories.

OF BIRDS AND BLOOD

The downstairs parlour was teeming with young German soldiers. Isabeau sneered at the sight. It was the price for staying open while Paris suffered under Nazi occupation: serve the German soldiers exclusively or be shut down.

Madame Vivienne had opted to cater to the Germans.

Most of the women who worked here wore military-styled clothing: tight skirts in German colours with matching bolero jackets decorated with braids and stars. Isabeau's harsh expression softened as her gaze flicked from woman to woman to woman. Her sisters, really, in spirit if not in blood. It was a bad time to be without work, without money. No, she decided finally—for the umpteenth time—Madame Vivienne had chosen correctly, protecting her girls.

Still, she didn't have to like it.

She lingered another moment, watching her sisters. Frowned. Stared harder into the shadowy corners. Brigitte was missing. Isabeau's breath caught in her throat, and she leaned over the railing to peer at the clock. Much too early to leave the parlour—Madame was very proud of her parties, the drinks and conversation and dancing, that reigned in the early evenings at her house. Private engagements happened later, after dinner.

Isabeau sighed, shoulders slumping. Marcelle had left early in the evening yesterday and hadn't returned. And Isabeau had heard rumours of other bordellos and missing women, too. And now Brigitte . . . ?

After a few seconds, Isabeau straightened with a shake. Despair wouldn't help anyone. It was her night off, and Andy, her disreputable Resistance friend, was expecting her, but she needed to act, to get information.

She smoothed her palms down her navy blue high-waisted shorts. A bit casual for Madame's parlour, but the brass buttons along the pockets gave the shorts the military flair that the boys seemed to like. She had paired them with a crimson blouse knotted at her waist, and Isabeau thought she looked wholesome.

Turning on a grin to hide her fear from the men, Isabeau trotted down the stairs and entered the parlour. Madame noticed her immediately, eyes narrowing and lips pressing into a thin line.

Isabeau greeted the server robot and plucked a crystal liqueur glass from the tray it held. Sipping the drink, Isabeau wended through the crowded room. A few hands caressed her hips and stroked her thighs, but Isabeau ignored them. The easy grin still lit her face when she reached Madame Vivienne's side.

"Well?" Madame asked.

"Brigitte. Did she go with *him*?" Isabeau demanded.

Madame shrugged. "It was her decision."

Isabeau's mouth went dry. Marcelle had gone with *him* last night, and no one had seen her since. Now Brigitte . . .

Hot tears filled her eyes. "You shouldn't have let her go."

Madame's mouth drooped, and for a moment, she looked weary and old. "He's called, asking for another. Brigitte wasn't"— her mouth twisted—"enough."

Oh, Brigitte. Isabeau swallowed. "I'll go."

Madame's eyes widened. "You cannot! I know about your young man. You cannot."

"I'll go," she repeated quietly. Passing on trivial German soldier gossip to Andy seemed insignificant in the light of the disappearance of another of her sisters.

A motor-car horn blared.

Madame sighed heavily. "He is here. Do as you will, Isabeau."

Isabeau nodded. Shoving sudden doubts and fears aside, she whirled around to cut through the very full parlour.

The night air was chill, and Isabeau shivered despite the feather-trimmed jacket she had grabbed on her way out the door. Parked in front of the bordello was a gleaming, six-wheeled, red motor car. It had a small cab—she doubted it could hold more than two people—and a long, cylindrical nose. Under the friendly light of the gas lamps, the grille of the motor car resembled a snarling, fanged maw. Isabeau shivered again, but not from the cold.

The window hissed open. "Please, come in," called a voice in German-accented French. *His* voice. The door clicked and swung upwards, like the hatch of a fighter plane.

Isabeau slid into the seat, the door gently swinging shut after her with another hiss.

A hand patted her bare thigh, and Isabeau turned her head, looking him full in the face.

Herr Fitcher. His flat black eyes gave her the creeps. His face was handsome, if stern and cold, with sharply defined features. Even though the faint odor of cologne perfumed the air, a heavy stubble shadowed his cheeks and chin, the hair so black that his skin looked grey in contrast. Privately, Isabeau and her sisters called him Bluebeard.

His thin lips curved into a faint, sardonic smile, the gleam of his teeth startling against his black-stubbled face. "Madame's parlour gets so crowded, and I prefer private conversation," Bluebeard said, squeezing her leg. "And I can tell I'll relish my time with you. What a beautiful bird you are." He leaned close and whispered in her ear, "You'll enjoy yourself at my home. Anything you ask, it's yours."

Isabeau summoned her parlour grin. "Sounds charming. It does get rather close in the parlour." Her heart thudded painfully, and she didn't ask about Brigitte.

Bluebeard squeezed her leg again and then settled back into his seat. He shifted the motor car into gear and the vehicle leaped away from the bordello.

The motor car devoured the road, and soon the city gave way to trees, but Isabeau could still see the twinkle of the lights. They weren't that far out of Paris. The motor car sped smoothly up a drive lined with elm trees, and ahead loomed a stone mansion. She nodded. Of course he would have commandeered a large house, not some cramped flat in the city.

When the motor car halted in front of the steps, Isabeau's door popped open. She climbed out and accepted Bluebeard's arm as they ascended the stairs, the sandy stone of the mansion glowing under the moonlight. The front doors were tall and rectangular, with a gold oval inset at the top. Slim, straight metal bars divided the bottom half of the glass doors into neat rectangles.

No one greeted them at the entrance, and Bluebeard took her feathered jacket and tossed it carelessly into a dark corner of the foyer. "Are you hungry?" he asked. "There's a sumptuous spread being prepared. I'm hosting a late dinner party this evening."

Her stomach gurgled in response, and he laughed. "Follow me."

They passed the massive, circular staircase that sprouted from the marble floor. Isabeau gawked at the beautiful iron railings, elegantly twisted into swirls. Splashes of gold highlighted the nodes where one swirl met another.

Bluebeard slid open a door farther down the hallway, revealing the dining room. Buffets and serving tables lined the walls, and in the centre of the room was a long, ebony dining table. The table was set with gilt-rimmed ivory plates, crystal glasses, and silverware. The food laid out on the serving boards stunned her. She'd never starved at Madame Vivienne's, but this! Several types of sliced meats, fruits, desserts, breads. The variety and amount were staggering. And there would undoubtably be hot foods, too.

Bluebeard waved her forward. "Please, help yourself." A clock *bong*ed, and Bluebeard frowned, pulling out a pocket watch.

"Damn, I've got to run." He planted a hard kiss on her mouth, mashing her lips against her teeth. "I've a meeting—our private conversation will have to wait."

His smile made her skin crawl. "What should I do while you're gone?"

"Whatever you'd like. Eat. Nap. There's a library on this floor somewhere, I've heard. Explore the house. But"—he held up a finger—"don't go in locked rooms. Those are off-limits. And one more thing"—he reached into a pocket—"keep this safe for me." He withdrew his fist and opened it to reveal a mechanical egg.

Isabeau heard the rough purr of some tiny engine. Bluebeard

pressed the top of the silver ovoid, triggering a hatch. Inside the egg, an ornate brass key nestled on black velvet.

"Don't lose it," he warned, still grinning. "Don't damage it. Don't get it dirty."

"I'll take good care of it," she said, dredging up a smile and cradling the egg in her hands.

After he strode from the room, Isabeau tucked the egg down the front of her blouse—it definitely wouldn't fit in her shorts pockets. The ovoid was surprisingly warm against her skin. Perhaps because of its small engine.

Isabeau had every intention of searching for Brigitte and Marcelle, but she didn't trust Bluebeard. She wouldn't put it past him to burst into the room after a minute or two, trying to catch her doing something sneaky. She filled a plate and ate methodically, her eyes fixed on the corner of the room where the massive grandfather clock squatted, rumbling as its engine pushed pistons and gears.

When enough time had passed, she started her search on the main floor, discovering the fabled library in her explorations. It was a beautiful room, facing the front lawns and driveway of the mansion. Bookshelves lined the walls. A solid desk dominated one end of the room, and a chaise longue was centred in the window. Heavy brass statues graced the end tables. Finding no sign of her sisters, Isabeau ascended the wide, winding staircase to the second floor. The metal railing was cold and smooth. In the dim light, the golden orbs adorning the railing were a comfort, providing an illusion of warmth.

When the second level proved also empty of people, she followed the curving staircase up to the third floor. Her pulse pounded painfully in her ears, and she could feel droplets of perspiration trickling along her hairline.

The third floor was very quiet. And empty, save for evenly spaced console tables. Crystal vases filled with fresh flowers adorned each end of each table, bracketing crystal candy dishes. Despite the eerie silence, Isabeau was convinced she'd find her sisters.

She stepped toward the first door and paused. Touched the ovoid. The silver egg still emitted heat; it hadn't cooled to match her body's temperature. Bluebeard's sinister grin as he handed her the egg seemed to float in front of her.

"Keep it safe, my eye," Isabeau muttered. It was some sort of grotesque test. He probably wanted her to break the damn thing. She pulled the egg out of her blouse and tucked it securely into a candy dish. She depressed the button and, when the hatch opened, plucked the key from its velvet nest.

It was the third door that wouldn't open. Isabeau rattled the knob a few times, but it was firmly closed and locked.

The key fit perfectly, and the door unlocked with a faint but precise click.

Recalling again Bluebeard's disturbing command, Isabeau stuffed the key into her tight shorts pocket and pushed the door open.

She didn't scream. Her hands flew to her mouth, holding in the bile that surged up her throat and flooded her mouth.

Blood.

Everywhere, blood.

Splatters on the wall, grotesque roses tainting the air with the stench of death.

Puddles on the floor, thick and tacky. One finger-like pool nudged her boot, and gagging, she jerked her foot back.

In the corner nearest her, an industrial washing basin, its shiny steel surface splotched with brown stains. Piled in the basin—

Gulping, Isabeau shut her eyes. She took a few deep breaths, forcing herself to calmness. She needed to make certain.

Steadier, she lowered her hands and crouched, swiftly removing her boots. She couldn't avoid the puddles of blood on the floor. Bluebeard had intended her to find this horrible abattoir, and the smallest bloodstain would betray her knowledge of this foul place. But she had to know.

Deftly, she tiptoed, side-stepping the puddles, and approached the basin. The remains of her sisters were piled haphazardly in the sink. They'd been hacked into pieces. At the bottom of the basin were two heads. Marcelle and Brigitte.

Their faces wore identical expressions of terror, eyes wide and mouths frozen into grimaces of fear.

"My sisters!" Isabeau wept, biting down on a sob as tears streamed down her face.

Her tears splashed onto the heads, smearing dried drops of blood. Isabeau stroked their matted hair. If only she could save them. Fix them. Weakly, she pushed the heads against ruined torsos. But the skin didn't magically knit together. Mewling, Isabeau turned away from the grisly contents of the sink.

Against the far wall, alongside a table holding strange scientific equipment and supplies, stood a row of silent and still metallic people. She stared at the gleaming gold humanoids. They were vaguely feminine, with filigreed metal framing the heads and the barest suggestions of breasts and hips. Robots? Far more sophisticated models than she'd ever seen. Focusing again on the basin and its terrible contents, Isabeau tugged the heads free and carried them to the robots.

And then stood there, helplessly, unsure of what to do. She wasn't an inventor nor a scientist. She was a heartbroken prostitute.

Isabeau took another deep breath and forced herself to study the equipment. Chemicals, flasks, cords, and wires. Large, empty canisters. A huge metal box. There was method to Bluebeard's madness. These weren't random tools.

"I will become an inventor," Isabeau murmured to the heads of Marcelle and Brigitte.

She put each head into one of the large canisters. From the canisters spiralled thick blue cords that attached to the metal box. The control box was covered with dials, gauges, and levers—and two large buttons. Out of the box, more cords twisted to the dais on which stood the robots.

She hadn't created these machines, but she intuited what they were supposed to do.

Isabeau flipped the levers into an "ON" position. The metal box began humming. Flicking nervous glances at both the robots and her sisters' heads in the canisters, Isabeau pressed the green button.

The canisters lit up. Her sisters' faces glistened from Isabeau's tears. They were radiant. Diamonds. Flashes of light burst and crackled inside the canisters. Brigitte's face softened, the terror-stricken expression smoothing out. Marcelle's face also gentled. Both women looked at peace. Almost serene.

The cords leading into and out of the giant metal box twitched and quivered.

Sparks flickered along the edges of the dais and up the motionless forms of the robots. A loud crash of static blasted from the control box. Then a blanket of silence settled over the equipment. The lights died; the cords sagged into stillness.

Isabeau stepped towards the golden robots. "Brigitte?" she whispered. "Marcelle?"

The eyes on two robots glowed orange.

"Isabeau?" asked one, its head swivelling uncertainly. It had Brigitte's voice.

"Brigitte!" Isabeau cried and dashed to the robot. She threw her arms around the stiff being and pressed her cheek against the slightly too-warm metal body.

"Isabeau?" the robot repeated. Metal arms awkwardly patted Isabeau's back. "It's not safe here! Did you drop the egg?"

"He'll punish you!" gasped the other robot in Marcelle's voice. "It can't get dirty! No blood!" She hiccoughed and sobbed.

"No blood," echoed Brigitte.

Isabeau gently extracted herself from Brigitte's embrace. "The egg is safe. It didn't get dirty."

"I dropped it," said Brigitte sadly, "when I saw what had happened to Marcelle."

Isabeau remembered her own moment of shock, when her body had flinched at the horrible sight of the room. She would have dropped the egg, too, if she'd been carrying it.

"I have to get you out of here," Isabeau said.

"But we're . . . dead?" Marcelle asked. She moved her arms, and her head tilted, examining her fingers as they curled and uncurled.

"Not exactly," Isabeau said. "I wanted to fix your bodies, but I couldn't. Instead, I transferred your souls into Bluebeard's robots."

"We're alive?" Brigitte asked.

"Metal bodies," Marcelle said. "*We* can punish *him*." Her eyes flared pumpkin orange.

Brigitte *hmm*ed thoughtfully.

"He deserves punishment, Marcelle, he does. But"—Isabeau held out a hand—"we have to do it carefully. So the Nazis don't destroy you a second time."

It was Marcelle's turn to *hmm*.

"Ah, you have a plan, Isabeau?" Brigitte asked.

Isabeau hesitated. As panic constricted her chest, an idea flashed into her head. She smiled slowly. "I do." She gazed around the room. "I'll need your help carrying some things downstairs."

The three women went downstairs—Isabeau stopping to wash her hands and feet, put her boots on, and to gather the silver egg. After preparing for Bluebeard's return, Brigitte and Marcelle went outside to where the motor car was still parked. Isabeau winced as their footsteps rang in the entryway, but nobody came to investigate.

Isabeau waited for Bluebeard.

He found her in the library, curled up on the chaise longue with a plate of fruit in her lap and a book propped on the arm of the chaise, the silver egg snug in her cleavage.

His black eyes glinted, but his smile was genial enough. "My little bird, I'm so happy you've made yourself comfortable."

He held out his hands, and Isabeau clasped them, allowing herself to be pulled to her feet.

"That is a unique holding place for my egg," he whispered. "May I have it back?"

She smiled and gave it to him. Bluebeard held it to the lamp and examined it and then opened the hatch and stared at the key. He grunted, mouth contorting with disappointment, before he recovered and smiled at her brightly.

"You've taken good care of it—not a blemish! I think"—he waggled his eyebrows—"you deserve a special treat."

Isabeau's smiled widened. "My treat should be your treat, too. Fetch another of my sisters from Madame Vivienne's. We'll have a really special time." She stood on tiptoe and stroked his lips with her index finger. "What do you say?"

He grabbed her hand and squeezed her fingers. "I say yes," he croaked. "I will send someone in my motor car. Unfortunately, my dinner party is to begin soon." He kissed each of her trapped fingertips. "Our special time will have to wait even longer. I'm sure you and your friend will find something to amuse yourselves?"

"Oh, yes," Isabeau purred. She lifted her chin in invitation, and he accepted, again crushing her lips in a hard kiss. The metallic tang of blood burned her tongue, but she moaned and wriggled against him. With her free hand, Isabeau reached behind her and grabbed the brass statue from the end table. She heaved it up and around, crashing it against Bluebeard's neck and head.

He cried out, releasing her hand. Bluebeard sagged to the floor, eyes fluttering. "What?" he asked. "Did you . . . ?"

Isabeau bared her teeth at him. "I found Brigitte and Marcelle, you monster," she hissed. "And you're going to pay for what you did."

His snake-like eyes sparked and he tried to regain his feet.

"Remember that I outsmarted you," she said as she swung the statue around again. This time he slumped to the floor and stayed there.

From the jerky movements of his chest, he still lived, but she couldn't count on him staying unconscious. Using the cords from the curtains and lamps, Isabeau tied him up to the heavy desk. She ripped apart a throw pillow and stuffed fabric in his mouth, tying a second strip of cloth over his mouth so he couldn't spit out the rag.

Satisfied that Bluebeard wasn't going anywhere soon, Isabeau left the library, closing the door firmly behind her. She trotted to the front entrance and opened the doors. The motor car was gone. She sighed and felt her shoulders relax. Brigitte and Marcelle were safely away, and she could proceed with the next part of the plan.

Returning to the library, Isabeau dragged another robot from under the desk. She heaved it onto the chaise longue and posed it, framing its head in the window. People approaching the mansion would see a young woman relaxing in the library. With the lamp turned down, Isabeau believed that anyone peeking into the library from the hallway would also be fooled for a few seconds.

Finally, she found her feathered jacket and went outside, taking up position at the bottom of the main staircase. Soon, motor cars started to arrive. They carried women dripping in jewels and furs and men in crisp, German military uniforms. From the bars and insignia, they were highly ranked officers.

Isabeau dutifully explained where the motor cars could be parked and directed the fancy men and women up the stairs to the mansion. Herr Fitcher, she explained, was overseeing the kitchen staff for the final preparations of the wonderful feast. He had even planned entertainment, she explained further, in a hushed tone, waving to the library window where the head of a young woman could clearly be seen.

After several minutes, the stream of cars dwindled. Isabeau directed the last arrivals into the mansion and then ran down the drive. It was cold this late at night, but she soon warmed up. When she reached the end of the drive, she turned onto the main road towards the city. Her pace slowed and she gasped for breath, but she didn't stop. She needed to put distance between herself and Bluebeard's grand mansion.

Several minutes later, planes roared overhead. Isabeau stopped and gazed upwards. The bombers were silvery phantoms in the purple-black sky. As hatches opened and bombs dropped, Isabeau laughed. Explosions ripped into the house, orange blossoms of fire shooting into the sky.

Brigitte and Marcelle had made it home and had found Andy. In turn, Andy, her friend in the Resistance, had reached his friends in the Royal Air Force.

Isabeau resumed walking. She would be able to report to Brigitte and Marcelle that Bluebeard had been punished. No more butchering and experimenting on women for him. And with a houseful of Nazi officers dead, Isabeau could see a glimmer of hope in the orange glow of the sky. The war wasn't over yet, but a happy ending awaited her and her sisters. She was sure of it.

THE COW'S IN THE MEADOW, THE BLOOD'S IN THE CORN

Originally published in *Blood & Water*, edited by Hayden Trenholm. Bundoran Press, 2012.

I am forever grateful to Hayden Trenholm for selecting this story for Blood & Water, *an Aurora-award winning anthology. It's my first published science fiction story. I would love to rewrite it—the temptation to do so for this collection was strong—but ultimately decided to leave it untouched. I am amused that my fascination for gadgets and weird western aesthetics is evident from the beginning.*

THE COW'S IN THE MEADOW, THE BLOOD'S IN THE CORN

A dense black cloud of flies buzzed over the carcass. A magpie cawed a warning to the insects, hopping across its claim as it peeled strips of flesh from the body. As it left one area unprotected, the flies descended, feasting until the magpie returned to chase them away. The dance would continue until a larger predator discovered the free meal.

Laura would have laughed at the intricate game played by the flies and bird if she hadn't seen the same display on four other cows this morning. She'd lost close to thirty cows in three weeks. She swept her flat-brimmed hat off and swiped at the bugs and bird, shrieking her own harsh threat. The magpie fluttered to a spot about a metre away and cocked its head at her, bright black eyes watching her with a fixed interest that would have given her the creeps if it had been human.

She knelt beside the cow and examined the wound at the neck. Straight and clean: a knife. "God dammit," she said. Laura removed her phone bud from her ear and snapped pictures of the wound, the cow, and the tattoo in the cow's ear. She'd have to identify the animal through her stud books. With an absent wave of her hat, she scattered the reforming cloud of flies and stared at the cow in grim silence for a few minutes before rising.

Laura activated the black phone bud and pushed it back into her ear. "Hey, Greg," she said in response to the gruff voice that greeted her. "I've got five cows that I need you to salvage."

She flapped at the flies again. "No, not for human consumption. The zoo again, if they'll take them."

Plopping the hat back on her head, Laura shooed away another wave of flies with her hands. "Right, thanks, Greg, see you in a few." Laura ended the call and took a couple more photos of the cow and the spray of blood discolouring the prairie grass. She jabbed a hot pink flag into the ground next to the corpse and returned to the barn.

The herd knew something was wrong; no doubt they could smell their slain sisters. The cows milled in the paddock, lowing nervously. They weren't eating. Laura cursed again. She didn't need the cows upset with breeding season coming up; they wouldn't catch. She frowned, wiping a sweaty palm on her jeans. She'd have to increase security around the bull barn. Her livelihood depended on Highland Laddie, her champion bull.

Murmuring a stream of soothing nonsense to the cows, Laura broke out a bale of pea hay and scattered it among the troughs. It didn't have a lot of nutritional value, but the cows loved it, and they deserved a treat with all the trauma of the past few weeks and the constant stench of blood hanging over the pasture.

The crunch of gravel announced Greg's arrival. Laura met him at the pasture gate. She unlocked it and pushed it open and Greg's old-fashioned pickup truck—it ran on diesel rather than the new corn ethanol fuel—drove into the field, the refrigerated compartment rigged to the bed swaying as the truck jounced over bumps and dips in the ground.

She waited for him at the gate, staring at the wide blue expanse of sky above, and mulled over who hated her so much that they'd kill cows. The corn farmers topped the list, but there were a few competitors who might feel threatened by her business. When the truck returned, Laura opened the gate again, closing and locking it after Greg had gone through.

Greg rolled down his window. "You sure you don't want this for yourself?"

Laura shook her head. "My freezer's full. Do you think the zoo will take them?"

"They took the others, and I don't see why they'd turn these down. Lions gotta eat every day too." Greg peeled off his cap, wiped his glistening forehead with his forearm, and smashed the cap back onto his head. "Laura, girl, you need more people watching your cattle at night, or you're gonna lose 'em all."

Laura's chin lifted. Asking for a punch, her father would have joked. "I don't have enough people, Greg. Everyone wants to get into corn."

"Your daddy would want me to help you out." He drummed his fingers on the steering wheel. Laura's eyes were drawn to the thick, gnarled knuckles. Greg was too old to babysit cows during the wee hours of the night.

"Look, Greg, there's no need—"

"Hush." Greg popped open his glove compartment and rummaged in it for several seconds. "Aha!" He leaned out his window and waved a small rectangle of paper at her.

Laura took it from him, rubbing a thumb over the soft, textured paper. She hadn't seen a physical business card in years. The ink had faded; she had to squint to make out the words. "MacDougall Security?"

"Yep. Give 'em a call." Greg tweaked the bill of his cap, put the truck in gear, and drove off. Laura watched until he had turned onto the main road, then went back into the barn.

Laura flipped the card over and over before abruptly coming to a decision. It took a few minutes to arrange for Charles, one of the ranch hands, to come down to the cow barn. While she waited for him, Laura went into her office and booted up her stud book. Responding to voice prompts, the computer accessed her phone's data and downloaded the photos. It found results almost immediately and displayed the matches for her approval. Laura sighed and recorded the date and cause of death of the cows, and how the bodies had been disposed. The computer chimed when it finished updating the cows' records.

"Save and shut down," Laura said, pushing out of her chair. She didn't wait for the computer's confirmation beep.

Charles stood at the corral in the main barn, bare arms propped on the beams, watching the cows dig for the remaining wisps of pea hay. Rivulets of sweat carved trenches on his dust-streaked face. The large ceiling fan spun at its highest speed, but did little to cool the barn's interior.

Laura gave Charles instructions for cleaning the bloodstained pasture grass and the cows' care for the day.

Charles nodded, pushing the brim of his hat up onto the crown of his head. "The cows will be fine, Laura. You go on into town."

A yellow-brown haze crowned Calgary, making the city one brown splotch from the ground to the sky. Even the Bow River, sluggish and dull these days, looked more like a ribbon of mud than of water. Laura wrinkled her nose. The blistering hot summer wasn't kind to Calgary; winter, with its thick blankets of snow, hid the city's flaws—the tall slabs of tenement buildings which had sprouted up to curb the city's sprawl, the shabby houses of the eastern quadrants.

The dashboard computer accessed maps of the city and programmed a route through the maze of one-way streets of the downtown core. Poverty had not breached this part of Calgary. Sleek skyscrapers brushed the sky with brassy arrogance. The logos on the buildings may have changed, but the people within them hadn't. Fuel was fuel, whether it was ethanol or oil, and there was money to be made.

In defiance of the heat outside, the receptionist of MacDougall Security wore a long-sleeved blouse and a chocolate brown wool skirt that complemented the peach and aqua decor. She arched her eyebrows at Laura. "Do you have an appointment?"

"No." Laura refused to look down at her plain cotton shirt and jeans. "I was in town and decided to stop by. Is Mr. MacDougall available? He was recommended by a friend of mine."

The woman sniffed. "I'll see, but don't be surprised if he's not. Mr. MacDougall is terribly busy."

"I'll wait, thanks." Laura sat on one of the plush, peach-coloured chairs, and picked up a reading tablet. Current issues of several magazines were loaded onto the device and Laura hummed as she scrolled through the list. Beneath her feet, she could feel the thrum of air conditioning working at full blast.

Laura knew what the answer was before the receptionist opened her mouth; her heels had a sullen click. "Mr. MacDougall can see you now."

"Thanks." Laura set down the tablet.

He waited for her inside the open door of his office. "Laura Lochlin? Greg called me earlier today, said you might drop by.

I'm Archie MacDougall."

Tall, with raven black hair, tanned skin, and sky-blue eyes, Archie MacDougall looked nothing like what she expected. Laura blinked, aware that she had been gawking at him. "Sorry," she said, "I was under the impression that you were a friend of Greg's." She took the hand he proffered and gave it a moderate squeeze, noting the lack of calluses.

Archie laughed. "He's an old friend of my dad. I've known him since I was a kid. Here, have a seat." He perched on the edge of his desk as she sat in the red leather chair. After a couple moments of silence, he said, "Greg mentioned trouble with your cows?"

Laura nodded. "Someone has killed twenty-seven of them in the past few weeks."

Archie whistled. "Any idea who?"

"Sort of," she said. "I have a lot of land and I don't use it to grow corn. I've had dozens of offers since I took over the ranch after my father died. Someone's trying to take my home and ruin my business."

"Pardon me for asking, but wouldn't corn be more profitable than cows?" His tone implied: *wouldn't corn be safer?*

Laura shrugged. "You'd think so, but with the shift in the corn market, there's a demand for cow products. For beef, sure, and I'd be lying if I said that most of my income didn't come from supplying high-end restaurants. But there're also medical uses for cow organs. And now . . . well, there isn't enough corn-based food for humans, let alone for grain-fed cows, not since the US started concentrating on ethanol production. That's why the Ontario beef market went under—they couldn't finish their cattle on corn grain." She leaned forward, eyes sparkling. "I have Sussex cows, able to survive drought, but they can also withstand the cold. They're just about perfect for the climate we have now in Calgary. Plus, they don't need fancy grain to produce good quality beef."

"Okay, so you raise cattle instead of growing corn, and someone is killing your cows to intimidate you into selling the land. Or drive you out of business if they can eliminate enough of your herd." Archie cocked his head. "Does that about sum it up?" When she nodded again, he said, "What security do you have now? Cameras? Retina-scanners on the barns and fences? Voice recognition locks?"

Laura worried her bottom lip, taking a perverse pleasure in the slight sting of pain. "Nothing."

"Nothing?" Archie glared at her. "Not even a dog?"

Her eyes widened. Pets, even working pets, were expensive, a luxury. In addition to affecting corn grain production, the US diversion of corn from food to fuel had impacted domestic pet food. Often used as filler for cheaper brands, the disappearance of corn had put a lot of the pet food manufacturers out of business. People with dogs and cats had to invest in organic vegetarian brands or the all-meat brands; those companies had jacked up the prices of their product. Dog and cat populations in animal shelters had ballooned as the number of abandoned pets soared.

"I have an arrangement with my butcher to send all the unused meat and bones to the Humane Society." Laura smiled. "In a way, I have dozens of dogs, but none of them live with me."

Archie muttered something and stood up, crossing to the other side of his desk. He slid open a panel, revealing a tablet which he then proceeded to manipulate, scrolling, typing, and pressing. After a few minutes, he swivelled the tablet around and showed her the screen. "It won't be cheap, and you may lose more cows, but I think we can catch the bastard."

"With that thing?" Laura's eyebrows shot up in surprise. "Are you serious?"

"Completely."

Laura braked, careful to bring the truck to a smooth halt so she wouldn't jolt the box beside her. It was a simple cardboard container, with a lid that folded into a handle and holes punched along the top, much like what pet stores used. Archie had said that the box was camouflage, meant to fool people.

Laura grabbed the handle and slid out of the truck, kicking the door shut. The barn was empty. Charles, she knew, would be out in the pasture with the cows while they grazed, and would guide them back to the barn at dusk.

Once the box rested on the desk in her office, Laura wiped damp palms on her jeans. Holding her breath, she peeled away the flaps of the box like it was an artichoke.

Within sat the mech cat, silent and motionless. Beneath the machine was an instruction booklet and a slim white cable. Laura pulled the booklet out from under the mech cat and flipped through the pages.

"This had better work," Laura said. She straightened her shoulders, cleared her throat, and said in a clear, slow voice, "Kitty. Wake."

The mech cat whirred. Eyes opened and ears twitched. Kitty stretched, first leaning back to work out the kinks in its front legs, then putting its weight on its front paws while it shook first one hind leg, then the other. Its tail pointed straight up. Only after the ritual was completed did the mech cat look at Laura. "Miaow."

Laura's hand hovered above the cat's head. Gulping, she gave the cat a nervous pat on the head. Beneath the realistic grey tabby fur, Laura felt the vibration of gears and motors. It was abnormally warm. It was close to being real, but just alien enough that her arms erupted in goose flesh.

Her mouth scrunching with an unvoiced "ew", Laura yanked her hand away with a shudder. "Good Kitty." Luckily, it would respond to vocal commands; there wasn't a need for her to touch the thing.

The mech cat purred. If she listened closely, Laura could detect the faintest of burrs in the sound, what she knew to be a hint of the mechanical workings of the device, but what anybody else would assume to be just a throaty purr. Archie had been right. The thing was worth every penny she had spent on it. There wasn't a question in Laura's mind that it would trick people, especially the fiends that kept killing her cattle. The mech cat would have more than enough time and opportunity for its visual, audio, and infrared sensors to record every movement of the villains.

Laura spent hours testing the mech cat's various security protocols, the clarity and efficacy of the sensors, and programming commands. Kitty did not have wireless capability for security purposes, but the company had included the cable to compensate. Laura linked Kitty with her stud registry computer, which had extensive maps of her property, and programmed a route for the mech cat to patrol at night.

When dusk fell, Laura put Kitty outside. "Patrol, Kitty."

"Miaow." Kitty strolled into the pasture with the languid confidence of a queen surveying her domain. Laura would have sworn it was a real cat.

Laura met Kitty at the barn before dawn. The mech cat purred and rose up on its hind legs, attempting to bump its head into Laura's palm for a pat. Laura flinched and stuffed her hands into her pockets. "Report, Kitty."

Kitty mewed and a flap of fur sagged away from its neck, revealing a data port. Laura grumbled as she hooked the mech cat up to the computer, her fingers fumbling with the unfamiliar cable. The upload was completed in a few seconds; the stud book displayed the mech cat's report. Zip, zero, zilch.

The barn door creaked. "Laura?" Charles called.

Laura yanked the cable out of the mech cat, tossed it under the desk, then bent over and pushed the skin flap back into place. "In my office!"

"Morning, Laura. What . . . is that a *cat*?"

Laura's fingers twitched. Gritting her teeth, she gave Kitty a nervous stroke along the neck, making sure the panel was closed. "Good Kitty." At the magic words, the mech cat mewed, stretched a hind leg, and hunched over its spine to lick its nether regions.

Laura straightened. "Yeah. A cat." She ran her tongue over dry, cracked lips. She hated lying. "It gets a little lonely, working in here all day, so I thought a pet would be nice."

"Sure." Charles scratched his head. "Aren't pets awfully dear though?"

"I own a ranch, Charles." Laura forced a laugh. "I'm not lacking meat, especially now."

"Oh." Charles eyed the mech cat with distaste. "Well, I was wondering if Highland Laddie should be brought down today. It's getting a little late in the season."

An icy tingle swept up Laura's back. Risking Highland Laddie, was this what the cow killer had been waiting for? The locks on the cow pasture and barns hadn't been a problem for whoever the villain was. She glanced down at Kitty. She did have the mech cat and all the hands would continue to watch the cattle at night. She gave an abrupt nod. "Yeah, let's move him down today and reacquaint him with the girls."

Shrill yowls woke Laura up. A fleeting glance at the clock told her it was nearly four in the morning—she'd only been asleep for an hour. Laura yanked on yesterday's jeans and socks and rammed her feet into boots. As she stumbled out of her bedroom, she jammed her phone bud into her ear.

Laura ran to the front door, grabbing the rifle that she'd placed there earlier, when her guard shift at the barn had ended. Kitty joined her and both jumped over the porch steps and sped towards the barn. Laura could see a strange truck parked by the building and she increased her pace. Kitty raced ahead, body stretched low over the ground, tabby fur blending into the grey shadows of approaching dawn.

Two men hunched over the lock on the barn door. With a shriek, Kitty launched itself at the nearest man, back claws sinking into the meat of his shoulder while its front claws raked his face. Screaming, Kitty's victim clutched at the mech cat and stumbled in a lopsided circle. The other man swore, dancing out of the way of his blinded partner, and flapped his arms at the mech cat. Kitty hissed and swiped at an arm, ears pressed flat against its head.

Laura skidded to a halt and raised her rifle, sliding the safety off. "Kitty, light!"

Eerie green light flooded the night. Even though she'd been expecting it, Laura flinched at the sight of Kitty's glowing orbs. The uninjured man shouted, one hand sketching a cross in the air.

"Kitty, come," Laura said. The mech cat detached its claws, hopped off its victim, and sauntered to Laura, its tail lashing the air. Kitty butted its head against Laura's knees before sitting at her feet, directing its green shafts of light at the two men.

The injured man lowered his hands from his face and Laura hissed. Charles. Keys glittered in the gravel at his feet. No wonder it had been so easy for the cow killers; they'd had inside help.

Laura kept the rifle pointed at them as she activated her ear bud and called the RCMP. She recognized the other man now, Hal Reynolds, one of the corn farmers who had tried to buy her land several times. Neither man spoke as she talked to the dispatcher.

"I hope you got something on these guys, Kitty," she said.

"Miaow." Kitty's mouth unhinged, giving the feline features a crocodile look.

"What the hell is that?" Charles asked, an edge of hysteria to his voice.

The faint hiss of white noise came from the mech cat, and then Charles' voice again, thinner and tinny.

". . . brought the bull down today on *my* say-so. He won't be no problem, he's pretty tame."

Hal Reynolds' voice next: "Be a bigger mess, though."

Both men laughed, the guffaws sounding like squawking crows through the mech cat's speakers.

"Thanks, Kitty. Sound off." Laura's hands clenched around the rifle, her knuckles showed white. "Why did you do this?"

"*Why?* You're wasting good land on cattle, that's why." Reynolds spat in the dirt.

A sour smile curled her mouth. "At least I'm feeding people. Your damned corn is feeding American cars, fattening up fuel barons." Laura flicked her eyes to Charles. "Where are the others?" Her gut tightened, waiting for his answer. Had she been betrayed by all of her men?

The bloody stripes on Charles' face made him look fierce. "I sent them to bed. Said it was almost light, nothing would happen." He shrugged.

Tension eased from Laura's shoulders. "Fine."

Headlight beams bounced down the drive. Laura kept the rifle trained on the two men until the Mounties had climbed out of their trucks and taken over. She levered the safety back on and excused herself. Then she ran to the barn.

The padlock dangled from the latch. Laura slipped it off and swung the door open, reaching with her right hand for the light switch. Even from the doorway she could pick out Highland Laddie's bulk amidst the cows. The bull lifted his sleek red head and blinked at her, lowing. At his call, the cows raised their heads, brown eyes sleepy and bewildered.

Laura smiled. The bull and the cows were fine. There would be calves next spring, and her herd would continue to thrive. She would keep her home.

Kitty rubbed against the back of her legs, its rough, whirring purr demanding attention. Laura crouched and scratched the cat's ears. "Hey, there, Kitty. We make a pretty good team, don't we?"

The cat's warm body felt good against her cold fingers.

THE ADVENTURE OF THE BRASS LAMP

Originally published in *Brave New Girls: Stories of Girls who Science and Scheme*, edited by Paige Daniels and Mary Fan. Brave New Girls, 2017.

I have several stories in the Brave New Girls anthology series, books geared towards upper middle-grade and young adult readers featuring teen-aged female protagonists solving problems and winning the day because of science! (Or technology, or math, or engineering.) A perfect vehicle for my steampunk tendencies. Carrie Wheelwright is a recurring character in my entries for the anthology series—a third one will be published in the summer of 2025—and "The Adventure of the Brass Lamp" is the first in the trilogy.

THE ADUENTURE OF THE BRASS LAMP

Vancouver, British Columbia, Canada
1890

Carrie wrapped her arms around Maria's legs and boosted the girl up, staggering under the unwieldy weight. The fine drizzle misting down from the grey Vancouver skies had made the garden stones slippery and the flower beds muddy. Her boots were sinking into the dirt.

She couldn't see much, holding Maria, but she could feel her friend wiggling, trying to find a solid perch on the narrow window ledge. Maria swayed in her grasp, and Carrie teetered to keep them both upright.

"Watch it, Maria!" Carrie hissed.

"Sorry, it's slippery!"

Carrie sighed. Of course. If the garden stones were slick, then so were the stone walls of the house. She hadn't factored the weather into her plan, beyond insisting that they wear trousers and wool coats. In addition to protecting them from the rain, trousers were more practical for climbing through windows. And, she had to admit, it was important to her to look as thief-like as possible while they broke into her father's study.

But having never scaled her home in the rain, she hadn't anticipated needing gloves for clinging to the stonework or learning how to not sink to her ankles in mud or developing a tolerance for the itchiness of damp tendrils of hair clinging to her face.

Maria settled on the ledge on her knees and began wrestling with the window, Carrie gripping her friend's legs to give her extra stabilization. Maria's hands slid off the window, and her legs twitched. One boot smacked Carrie in the chin, snapping her head back. She grunted.

"Sorry!"

Carrie averted her face. Her jaw ached, and she would be amazed if a bruise didn't form. She sighed again, her mother's lecture on hoydens and proper behaviour and why-couldn't-she-behave-more-like-her-sister-Louisa already ringing in her ears.

And the worst of it was that her mother would have had a point. Carrie was burgling her own home, after all, an inexcusable action. But if it would prove to her father that her anti-burglary invention worked and was useful—well, that was worth a bruise and lecture.

Her father. He hadn't even tested the anti-burglary device. He'd called it frivolous, clunky, not worth developing. She ground her teeth together. It was a good idea. The window rattled above her, and she glanced up. Maria hadn't worked it open yet, however, so Carrie averted her face again, still seething.

The window rattled once more, and Carrie frowned. She hadn't counted on so much noise. If they woke people up before they triggered the anti-burglary device, the experiment would be for naught. And because her parents were hosting a house party for her father's potential investors, there were more people than usual to worry about waking: in addition to her parents, sister, and the servants, there were a couple of men from the Royal Canadian Navy; Mr. Dawson from the Hudson's Bay Company; and his assistant, Peter, a fish-eyed young man that Louisa seemed to fancy. He paid a lot of calls to the house, not always on business for Mr. Dawson and the HBC.

The benefit of the house party was that Carrie had been allowed a guest, too. Maria was her oldest and dearest friend, and they had been in all sorts of scrapes together—not all at Carrie's behest either, despite what her mother believed.

The window squealed and slid open. "All right," Maria called, "you can let go of my legs!"

Relinquishing her grip, Carrie took a step back from the window and watched her friend push aside the curtains, swing her legs over the sill, and disappear into the room.

Almost immediately, Maria's head poked back out the window. "Carrie, you need to see this!"

Responding to the urgency in Maria's voice, Carrie grabbed the ledge and kicked against the wall, which gave her enough momentum to haul her body over the ledge. She paused there, half-in and half-out the window, legs dangling. "Good thing I wore trousers," she muttered, before bracing her knees against the ledge and launching herself into the room. She landed in an ungainly heap on the carpet.

Carrie took a few seconds to sort out various aches and pains— the alarming twinge in her side was her tool belt poking her hip, not a broken bone—before accepting Maria's help to stand up. A quick scan of the room provided several disturbing details: the wall safe, ajar, with papers hanging over the edge; the strobing, gurgling brass desk lamp; and the desk on which the lamp sat, its drawers and contents strewn across the floor.

Someone had already burgled her father's study.

Paralyzed only for an instant with shock, Carrie raced to the desk and hit the off switch for the lamp's whistle. A former oil lamp with brass base and body and a white porcelain shade, the whistle tubing and delicate spout had been woven into the brass base of the lamp to conceal their function. Yet it had been dented, deliberately ruined! She'd have to use different materials for future models. Metals that wouldn't bend so easily. Or perhaps she'd have to create the entire base herself, giving the whistle system additional support . . .

Shaking her head to dislodge the distracting thoughts on metals, she next turned off the strobing light, making note to replace the incandescent bulb. Edison's invention was marvellous, but the bulbs didn't last long. Despite the fading bulb and the damaged whistle, Carrie smiled. "It worked," she whispered with a burst of pride. "It is worthy of development, Father."

"Did it break?" Maria asked, joining Carrie at the desk.

"No," Carrie said. "It's a little dented, but not destroyed. Did you see who triggered it?"

Maria shook her head, her long, black braid thumping against her shoulders. "The door," she said, pointing, "was just closing." She poked Carrie in the side. "Whoever it was, they must have worked fast. It's thoroughly ransacked, but nobody was in here when we went outside."

Carrie nodded. Someone already in the house had raided her father's study. She surveyed the mess with dismay, her joy in her anti-burglary device ebbing.

"I wonder what they took?" Maria asked, glancing around the room. "Does he keep jewelry in the safe?"

Carrie shrugged. "I suppose there's money in the—Oh." Her frantic gaze swept the desk. "Oh no." She knelt and ruffled the papers littering the floor.

Maria knelt beside her. "What?"

"The submersible plans! That's what's stolen!" Carrie stared at the clutter, willing the familiar plans to appear in the mess. The submersible would guarantee Father's status as a premier inventor, as well as providing the family with a generous income. He'd been courted for weeks by different departments of the Canadian government and several private companies—there had even been a secretive visit from Americans and telegrams in languages unfamiliar to her.

In addition to the immediate humiliation and ruination, there could be intangible consequences to the theft. Her father's reputation would affect them all. How would she make a career as an inventor if her father was labelled gullible at best and treasonous at worst? She wouldn't. Not easily.

The inside of her mouth tasted ashy. Carrie grimaced and stood. "Help me with the lamp, Maria. There's something I need to check."

Pulling a screwdriver from her tool belt, Carrie tipped the lamp to one side so that she could access the panels secreted in the main body of the lamp. Maria steadied the heavy lamp while Carrie manipulated the tool.

"I almost forgot," Carrie explained as she popped out a screw, "that I installed a camera. The tubing necessary for the whistle has been so difficult to design that I haven't tested the camera or its shuttering mechanism much, but it may have snapped a photochrome." Another screw twirled out, and the panel sagged open. Carrie pried out a small plate and slipped it into a pouch on her tool belt, then screwed the panel back into place. Together, she and Maria returned the lamp to its upright position.

"Let's go process the plate," Carrie said. "It won't take long."

"Process the plate?" Maria repeated. "Aren't we telling somebody about the theft? What about your father?"

"I'm not worrying my father about this, not when I can present him with the plans and the thief!"

Maria trailed her to the door. "The thief is probably on the other side of the door, waiting to bash our brains in!"

Carrie glanced over her shoulder, arching an eyebrow. "You've been reading too many pulps, Maria. The thief is cowering in his room, waiting for a great hue and cry to go up, and I'll not satisfy him." She put a finger to her lips. "If we're quiet, we can have this all figured out soon." *Our reputations will be secure, and Father will laud the success of my invention*, she thought.

Carrie hopped out of her dark room, fluttering the photochrome between two fingers. Converting the old wardrobe to a tiny dark room had been one of her best ideas. "Maria, look at our clue!"

Maria was tucked into a chair in front of the fireplace. When she didn't receive a response, Carrie walked around the chair and stifled a chuckle. Maria was asleep, cheek cradled in the palm of her hand. Strands of hair had escaped her braid, obscuring her face.

It was late, Carrie conceded, glancing at the intricate gaslight clock on the mantel. But the urge to prove the value of her device and secure her future had her brain buzzing like a hive of disturbed bees. She couldn't possibly sleep, not with the puzzle of the stolen plans still to be solved.

Better to put her agitated brain to work and present her father with a solution. Everyone would be happy: her father, for having his plans returned, and Carrie, for having foiled the plot with the use of her anti-burglary device. Even her mother would be happy, because staying up late would create dark circles under Carrie's eyes, and her mother would have another lecture topic. And Louisa would be happy to be left alone to her own interests, which seemed to be dresses, tea parties, and fish-eyed young men.

Carrie sank to the floor at Maria's feet and placed the photochrome gently onto the carpet. The red glow of the banked coals cast an eerie light over the black-and-white image.

It wasn't a particularly good picture. Too much light and the movement of the photochrome's subject had caused fuzziness and blurriness in places. Still, the hidden camera had managed to produce one clear item in the otherwise useless image: a maple leaf.

Carrie traced the maple leaf with a finger, humming absently as she thought. The Naval admiral had worn his dress uniform to dinner that evening; his shoulder had been adorned with maple leaves.

After deciding to let her friend sleep, Carrie carefully rotated a delicate scroll carved into the elaborate stone fireplace. The knot slid out, and Carrie reached into the exposed cavity, bringing out a large, ornate key. A skeleton key. She had filched it years ago—nobody knew she had it—and it had proved useful. With it she had access to all the rooms.

She'd been reading a scientific treatise when her mother had discussed room arrangements with Mrs. Potts and the butler, but Carrie knew her mother well enough to know which room would be given to an admiral in the RCN.

Around her head, she fastened a small gaslight, which rested against her forehead. It was a gadget of her own design, basically a miniature lamp, with a thick cloth pad protecting her skin. It would provide light for about an hour, useful for short adventures, and allow her the use of both hands.

She crept down the hallway, avoiding the creaky spots in the floor with the ease of long practice. At the door of the Grey Room, she stopped. Carrie inserted the key into the lock, turned it, and, taking a deep breath, pushed the door open.

The breath whooshed out of her as she was knocked down. Glass tinkled where her head lamp crashed against the floor. She lay stunned, a great weight pinning her to the floor.

"I've got you. Ha, I knew it!" a male voice said into her ear. "Hold still."

The weight lifted from her, but Carrie was too dazed to move. Her brain, recovering from the unexpected collision, feverishly processed the new information. The voice, not gruff enough to be the admiral . . .

"Lieutenant?" she asked. Why on earth had her mother

assigned the Grey Room to the lowly lieutenant?

"You're a— You can't be a girl?" came the man's voice. There was a scratch-hiss sound of a match being struck, and then the room was illuminated by the soft glow of a candle.

A young man—the lieutenant, still in uniform—sat on the bed, his jaw slack and eyes wide.

"You are a girl! But . . ." His mouth snapped shut, and he eyed her sharply. "Hang on, you are Dr. Wheelwright's daughter, aren't you?" He scowled.

Carrie sat up, feeling her head with tentative fingers. "Yes, I'm Carrie," she said, unfastening the head-lamp's band and lifting it from her head with careful and precise movements.

She cradled the mangled device in her hands. "You broke my head-lamp."

"Was that the noise?" The lieutenant came to her side, the candlestick in one hand. "Here, hold still," he ordered. "There's glass in your hair."

Gentle fingers raked over her scalp and combed through her hair, picking out shards of glass. After a few minutes, the fingers stilled and left her head.

"I think that's all." He sat back on his heels. "Now, what the blue blazes were you doing?" He shook his head. "I told the admiral something fishy was going on. This submersible deal has turned everyone crazy. I made him switch rooms with me." He scowled again. "I thought it would be the Russian, coming to strike a deal with the admiral, not the inventor's daughter."

"Russian?" She pictured each of the houseguests. She didn't recall a Russian.

"One of the men from the HBC. They'd love to have a submersible for exploring the Arctic. Checks out on the surface, but there's no denying he's Russian." He hesitated before adding, "The Russians living in Alaska weren't treated well when it was sold to the Americans. They were evicted."

Interesting. She filed that fact away. There were two men from the Hudson's Bay Company at the house. Her father had known Mr. Dawson for years. He always stopped by when he was in the city. The other man . . . "Do you mean Fish-Eyes? Er, Peter?"

"Yes. Peter Pavlovich." He shrugged. "It's no secret what your father's been working on. We know the Americans have visited your father. And the HBC has been here a lot—"

"Not the HBC," Carrie said slowly, a heavy feeling of dread creeping through her. "Peter."

"Pavlovich, HBC, it's all the same—"

"It's not the same!" she blurted. "It's not the same at all, Lieutenant Whoever-You-Are!"

"My name," he said stiffly, "is Franklin Beauchamp."

"My point," Carrie said, scrambling to her feet, "is that the HBC has not been here 'a lot', as you say. Not officially. But Peter has." She stroked her tool belt, drawing comfort from its solid weight as her thoughts reached a disturbing conclusion. "Visiting my sister."

Franklin stood up too. "Well . . . your sister . . ." He mumbled something about "attractive" and "only natural".

Carrie snorted. Maybe it was natural for Peter Fish-Eyes to court Louisa, but what did Louisa see in him? He had never impressed Carrie with his intellect. As a matter of fact, Peter Fish-Eyes still required help to find his way around the house.

Which means that he isn't the thief, she thought. He wouldn't have been able to find the study in the first place, let alone find his way back to his bedroom—she and Maria would have discovered him wandering the halls. She groaned. Eliminating Fish-Eyes as a suspect allowed a better interpretation of the clues she had gathered. Oh, Louisa.

Carrie grabbed Franklin's arm and gave him a shake. "I've made a mistake! The plans have been stolen, but we still have time to stop the thief!"

She turned, dragging him with her, and snagged her key as they exited the Grey Room. She missed her lamp, but she could still navigate the hallway in the dark. Especially since her destination was familiar.

"Did you say stolen?" Franklin whispered, stumbling behind her.

Carrie didn't hesitate when she reached the room. She stabbed the key in the lock and shoved the door open.

The room was much like her own, with the furnishings arranged in the same pattern. Her sister, Louisa, rose from a chair in front of her fireplace. "You're later than I expected. I thought you inherited the brains."

"Your sister?" Franklin hissed.

Carrie squeezed his hand. "I misinterpreted the clue," she said to Louisa. "Or rather, I didn't take into account all the clues." She dug into one of her tool belt pouches and pulled out the photochrome.

Louisa stretched out her hand, as if she were a noble lady receiving a peasant. After a few moments, Carrie approached her sister and held out the photochrome, which Louisa poked. "Where did you get that?" she mused, one eyebrow arching in surprise. A flash of annoyance chased the wonder from her face. "That infernal device! I thought I'd disabled it!"

Franklin released Carrie's hand and took the photochrome from her. "A maple leaf?"

Carrie felt a blush warming her cheeks. "I thought it was the admiral's insignia, but it's Louisa's brooch. An error on my part, leaving my family members off the suspect list."

Her sister's hand flew to her throat, where a delicate, golden maple leaf was pinned to the collar of her blouse.

Carrie sighed. "And I should have also realized that only a family member could have disabled my invention. No one else knows it exists. An outsider would have just seen an old, brass lamp." She forced a smile. "Where are the plans, Louisa?"

Louisa's lips curled. "I don't have them."

Franklin muttered something and ran out of the room.

Carrie didn't watch him leave; her gaze remained fixed on Louisa. "This will crush Father. Why did you do it?"

Louisa laughed. It was bitter and hateful sounding, shards of glass slicing the air. "I loathe this dirty town. And you and Father! Grit and grease under your nails, like common workers." Her eyes flashed, and an angry red stain spread across her face. "People see that grease and assume it's on me, too!"

"You're going to ruin our lives because of your social status?" Carrie blinked at her sister. "But you go to lots of parties, have many friends and admirers . . ."

Louisa sneered. "I am welcome at the homes of a bunch of dirty unsophisticates. I can be more."

"With Peter," Carrie said dully. She could hear doors slamming, voices, pounding footsteps.

"Peter's family lost their land with the sale of Alaska," Louisa said. "With the submersible plans, he can rebuild his family fortunes. The Tsar is interested in building Russia's navy. A secret, submerged navy that will bring him power and prestige—which will be shared with Peter. I," she continued dreamily, "will be part of the nobility."

"You—you selfish idiot!" Carrie yelled, suddenly enraged at her sister. "You can't possibly believe he's going to marry you!"

"You don't know anything about men," Louisa spat.

Carrie fingered her tool belt. "Peter's left then? With the plans?"

"Of course." Louisa lifted her chin. "He'll send for me."

Carrie stared hard at her sister. Louisa didn't seem the least bothered by her traitorous act. Even now, she remained defiant, cutting a dramatic figure in front of the fireplace. Carrie smiled. Her sister had forgotten who she was talking to.

Nodding, Carrie yanked her screwdriver off her tool belt and threw it into the fireplace. Sparks flew out from the coals, and Louisa shrieked, shielding her face with her arms. Carrie darted forward and twirled a stone scroll, twin to the one in her own room. It came loose easily, and she pulled out the item hidden within: a thick, folded square of blue paper. Carrie instantly recognized her father's neat notations. The submersible plans!

Louisa shrieked again, infuriated this time, and jumped at Carrie. Twisting out of her sister's grasp, Carrie ran for the door, fumbling at her tool belt. Prying open another pouch, she grabbed a handful of cogs and gears and tossed them behind her.

Her sister's cry of pain and the sound of her falling brought Carrie to a halt. She turned around, one hand curled around a new pouch on her belt.

Louisa sat on the floor like a deflated airship, clutching one foot which had a gear stuck in the sole. A shallow scratch blazed red on her cheek. She moaned, tears trickling down her face.

A twinge of pity tugged at Carrie's heart. She couldn't risk the plans, but she knew the household had been alerted by Franklin. She could afford an act of kindness toward her sister. Help was nearby if she needed it. Slowly, she stuffed the folded plans into a pouch on her belt. Then she walked back to her sister, helping her into the chair, mindful of Louisa's long fingernails.

"We'd best have the doctor brought round for that foot,"

Carrie said, propping it on a footstool. "I'll ring for a servant."

"Not necessary, Caroline. We've already sent for a doctor."

Carrie grinned and looked up. "Father!"

Louisa wailed, and the grin faded from Carrie's face. "Father, I've such a lot to tell you."

He strode into the room, tall and sturdy, with fierce moustache and chops. His eyes, even tired, were shrewd. "I've heard enough from Lieutenant Beauchamp. The entire household is in an uproar, tracking down that scoundrel, Peter. It's late, and you need your sleep." He fished a handkerchief from a pocket and offered it to his eldest daughter, who seized it and buried her face into it.

Dr. Wheelwright patted Louisa on the shoulder. "Now, Caroline, I presume you have the plans?" At her nod, he grunted in satisfaction. "I didn't think Louisa would be so foolish as to give those plans away before she got what she wanted."

Carrie shook her head. "Not even in love would Louisa be that daft."

A damp, bitter "Thanks!" came from the depths of the sodden handkerchief.

"Caroline," her father said, "you keep the plans tonight. And get to bed." At her hesitation, he added quietly, "Louisa will be fine. She'll need us tonight and in the coming weeks, but she'll be fine."

A heavy weight, one that had been sitting in her stomach since she'd realized Louisa must be the thief, dissolved. She had done her part, revealed the plot, retrieved the plans, and kept her father's reputation intact. Her parents could worry about punishment and smoothing the ruffled feathers of the Navy. "Good night, Father. Good night, Louisa."

"Good—oh, Caroline, let's go to the patent office tomorrow. I was clearly wrong, and your anti-burglary device shows real promise." He stooped to tend to the fireplace, signalling the end to the conversation.

It wasn't the grovelling concession she had dreamed of, but it was an acknowledgement of her invention's worth, which was what she'd really needed. "Thank you, Father."

Keeping one hand on the pouch containing the plans, Carrie hurried from the room, grabbing her skeleton key from the door.

Her steps slowed, and her brow wrinkled. She couldn't possibly go to the patent office without fixing a few things on the anti-burglary device. The whistle tubing and spout needed to be repaired and improved; the camera had been terribly neglected in the first prototype; and the light bulb! It needed to be changed.

As the list of repairs and modifications increased, Carrie started humming. She wondered how much she could get done tonight without waking Maria. She had never felt less tired.

OUTTA LUCK

Originally published in *Andromeda Spaceways Inflight Magazine*, n.57, 2013.

My first magazine sale, "Outta Luck" is an odd story, not fitting neatly into any one genre. Is it Weird West? Steampunk? Dystopic? Aliens? I'm not entirely sure, but it was fun to write. A second story featuring Hanna the smuggler can also be found in this collection.

OUTTA LUCK

Camels were smelly, stubborn beasts. Hanna shifted in her saddle, wincing. And damned uncomfortable. Unfortunately, the animals were now the only form of travel allowed in the desert bordering the country of Khazad. Hours after accepting her current job, Khazad had declared mechanical travel impure, banning it within its borders, and she hadn't been able to book passage on a motorized caravan in the allotted time frame. If Hanna had known about the soon-to-be-limited travel options, she would have refused the job. No amount of money was worth being spat on by a camel.

She snorted. Who was she kidding? She would have taken the job under any circumstances. Going to Khazad on a lark was unthinkable, but with somebody else footing the bill it was too good of an opportunity to pass up. The return job could rake in enough money for her to buy a house on Ciscan Bay—maybe retire from the smuggling game entirely.

Hanna spotted one of the Gelassians nudging her camel forward and grimaced. The three-day journey was coming to a close, and she was growing weary of her clients. Only the thought of the final payment, and the lucrative return job she had planned in Khazad City, kept her from spurring her camel into a gallop and abandoning the Gelassians. She twisted her expression into a smile when the camel settled beside her.

The rider sat her camel with a stiff back, her body unyielding to the rolling gait of the beast. She raised a hand in greeting. "How much longer?"

Hanna squinted into the glare of the sun. Her goggles had become so scratched during a sudden sandstorm on their first day out that they were now good for nothing but anchoring a linen scarf to her wide, flat brimmed hat. A dark haze was visible on the horizon, but an accurate judge of distance was impossible due to the unchanging landscape. Even her spyglass was useless in this terrain. She shrugged. "About an hour."

"You have the papers for the gate?"

Hanna could almost see an anxious frown on the Gelassian's face, even through the veil. "Are Khazadian saffron fields heavily guarded?"

The Gelassian woman didn't laugh.

Gods, what an uptight species. Giving the Gelassians coal would probably be a quicker way to earn a fortune—after a few days in their hands, she'd have diamonds. Hanna sighed. "Relax. There won't be a problem with the guards."

The woman's hands fluttered. "You are certain?"

Gelassians were sticklers for the rules. But because of Khazad superstitions, Gelassians as a race were barred entry into the city, forcing them to break all kinds of laws to get into the country. Gelassians weren't the only beings that the Khazad considered impure either—certain religious sects, criminals, and redheads were also discriminated against. Hanna wouldn't be shocked if men named Fred were banned.

"The documents are the best money can buy. You and your people will pass the purity requirements." Hanna *had* inflated the price of said documents, and the extra funds *had* found their way to her pocket, but the documents *were* of excellent quality. "Especially disguised as Bezal monks."

The female fingered the veil that covered her head and milk-white face. Her shoulders sagged for an instant. "Good," she sighed, "we've waited years to see the City."

She straightened almost immediately, her posture once again ramrod stiff, invulnerable. Her eyes glinted behind her goggles. "You won't receive the rest of your payment until after we've passed through the gates." Her camel decreased its pace, falling behind Hanna.

From now on Hanna would stick to smuggling goods that couldn't talk back.

About an hour later, Hanna and her camel train approached the massive gates of Khazad. A cluster of green minarets thrust up from the centre of the walled city, a dome of pinkish gold at its heart. Towers framed the gates; Hanna discerned the glimmer of metal in the darkened windows. Cannons, she surmised, to enforce the new travel laws. The presence of artillery was more than a little disconcerting, given the Khazadian distrust of explosive powder. They preferred edged weapons.

Jabbering in excitement, the dozen Gelassians milled behind Hanna. Not many outsiders saw the fabled Coral Palace of Khazad and the white limestone walls, or shopped at the exotic spice markets.

Hanna smirked. Some of those spices commanded a higher price than gold on the open market, let alone the black one.

Then several of the Gelassians whipped out handheld cameras. Brilliant flashes popped around them. Hanna frowned. The Khazadians' wariness of explosive powder extended to the benign amounts used for the photographic devices.

Hanna nudged her camel closer to her charges. "Put those cameras away! Khazad has strict laws about taking photographs. Wait until you're inside with the other tourists for that stuff.

"Are all your veils fastened properly? The purity papers aren't worth a damn if your clothes fail inspection. The Holy Order of Bezal doesn't expose skin." She guided her camel through the group, checking the veil ties and looking for worn spots on gloves and boots. Their skull-caps and goggles were tight, ensuring that not even a wisp of hair saw the light of day.

Satisfied, Hanna circled her camel around to face the city. "Let me do all the talking. Not a peep from any of you, understand?"

Now to earn that fee, paid in lovely gold nuggets.

She loosened the linen scarf wrapped around her own head as her camel halted in front of the gate. She smiled at the guards. "Good day to you, honoured sirs!"

"Papers," one grunted, holding out a hand.

"Of course, I have them right here." Hanna pulled a sheaf of papers from her satchel, her smile faltering as sand trickled off the sheets. The crisp white paper—expensive, hard to come by, and necessary to impress the guards—was now mottled and torn; the beautiful blood-red wax seals were scuffed and blurred.

Hanna poked a finger in her satchel. A hole! A hole in her supple, oiled leather satchel. The bottom of the bag was filled with fine, golden-hued sand.

Forcing the confident smile back upon her face, she handed over the tattered papers. Hanna remained relaxed, still smiling, as the guard scrutinized every sheet.

"Your papers are unclean," he said.

Hanna tapped the scratched and dinged goggles atop her head. "A sandstorm hit us on our way to your magnificent city, and I'm afraid our personal effects suffered for it." She leaned forward and whispered, "I had to sit for hours with a blindfold on while my Bezal clients repaired their garments."

"To see their skin is to be struck blind." The guard lowered his voice. "The merchants desire their patronage, though, so we are *obliged* to allow their entrance." Bending his head to hide the bitter spark in his eyes, he continued his perusal of the papers.

Hanna sat back in her saddle, smile in place. The Holy Order of Bezal was so fastidious about covering every inch of their body that all sorts of rumours had sprung up about the custom. Unless the Gelassians raised a doubt about their false identities, the guards wouldn't poke at the outfits.

Not that the guards would be sloppy. The second guard threaded through the camel train, one hand resting on his sword hilt. Hanna knew that his sharp gaze would notice the smallest inconsistency. The merest glimpse of the distinctive Gelassian skin would result in banishment . . . or worse.

The minutes ticked by. Hanna could feel her smile stiffening. They weren't going to buy it. She yawned. Feigning an itch, one hand crept beneath her desert travel robe and caressed the butt of her hand cannon. In Khazad, justice was swift and harsh, and she wasn't prepared to lose appendages for a bunch of gawky tourists.

The guard handed back the papers. "I'm not sure what a respectable woman like yourself is doing with a bunch of Bezal zealots, but please enjoy your stay in our city."

"Thank you, noble guardsman. I appreciate your *thorough* examination." Hanna batted her eyelashes at him. Her hand drifted away from the concealed weapon. "You can't be too careful, right?"

The guard nodded. "It's dangerous to admit certain types of people. Redheads are notoriously unlucky."

Typical Khazad bunk. "I've heard that about the Gelassians too," she cooed. "When will you be off shift? Maybe I'll be able to sneak away later."

The guard stammered a reply, and with another warm smile, Hanna led her troupe through the city gates, which creaked shut behind them.

They paused on the other side. The Gelassians let out a collective "ah". Throngs of people choked the narrow streets lined with stalls and vendors' carts. The Gelassians took their cameras back out with what they probably considered to be stealthy movements. Hanna rolled her eyes and pretended not to notice.

Their spokeswoman approached Hanna once more and handed over a small, heavy bag. "Thank you for your assistance. Here is the final instalment of your fee."

Hanna hefted the bag. She glanced up at the shadowed windows of the guard towers, chewed her lip, and tucked the bag into her satchel. "Good luck with your visit. Don't let the veils slip."

The Gelassians dismounted and led their camels through the crowded streets. As they passed a fruit stand, the cart buckled, spilling its contents all over the street. They shuttered a photograph of a small boy holding a donkey, which then kicked the boy and ran down the street, braying maniacally. A thief grabbed a few kebabs at the stall where they stopped to purchase food.

Hanna fingered the hole in her satchel while she watched the small disasters that followed the Gelassians down the street. Her own recent streak of calamities paraded through her mind: travel bans, freak sandstorm, scratched goggles, damaged documents.

She whistled. Blue blazes! The Khazadians had it right—the Gelassians *were* unlucky!

She hauled her camel around. It was a good thing her association with them had come to an end; she didn't want her return job jinxed.

The crooked streets of Khazad wove through the buildings like a river flowing through the mountains. It took Hanna a while to find the fleabag inn her contacts back in Port Angels had recommended. She dumped the camel off at the stable, then went inside to get a room.

The innkeeper was thin and greasy. He bowed and quoted an exorbitant price. Hanna grimaced. She had been warned about the outrageous Khazadian prices, which she suspected was an attempt to discourage sweaty people and their grubby children from visiting the city. Khazad wanted the wealthy to visit, but not to linger. The cost of a room in this hovel would get her a suite at a private resort in Ciscan Bay.

After an intense bout of haggling, Hanna whittled the price down to an amount she could live with. It was still highway robbery, but at least it was a dirt paved highway instead of a golden one.

Hanna clenched her jaw and reached into the satchel. Loosening the drawstring of the bag given to her by the Gelassians, Hanna slipped her hand inside and fiddled with the contents. She froze.

"Something wrong, mistress?" the innkeeper asked. He leaned close to her, lowering his voice. "If the price is not to your liking, you can try drinking yourself into a stupor at a tavern. The guards hold drunks in the jail overnight. You'd best get drinking soon though if you want a bed." An oily grin parted his lips, revealing a gumline that reminded Hanna of a piano keyboard, yellowing ivory keys alternating with ebony strips. "Or maybe we could reach some other arrangement."

"No thanks," she said. Reminding herself of the return job, of owning an *entire house* on Ciscan Bay, she bared her teeth in a semblance of a smile, repressing a shudder. "Nothing's wrong with the price we agreed on." Nothing was wrong at all, except for the bag full of coins stamped with the Gelassian coat of arms instead of safely anonymous gold nuggets. They'd cheated her! She should have risked catching the attention of the guards and verified her payment at the gate.

Hanna wasn't unprepared for such a difficulty, however. She reached beneath her desert robe to her leather vest, which had pockets sewn into the lining. Brushing aside her pocket watch, she removed a small gemstone and offered it to the innkeeper, careful not to touch his hand.

He held it up to his eye, then bit it. He grunted. "It will do."

The room was the pits. Dusty, with a faint odor of sweat and hashish, the room looked like it belonged in an abandoned house rather than an inn. It did have a bed—Hanna promised herself not to think about what might be living in the straw mattress—and a wash basin perched on a wobbly table. More than one cockroach scurried across the floor as she rummaged through her saddlebags, checking to see what else had been damaged in the desert crossing.

She removed the Gelassians' payment and scowled at the coins in the bag. The twits. She couldn't spend them here. She couldn't even exchange them for the local currency. Tossing the bag aside, Hanna next took out a brass tube. With a practiced flick of her wrist, the spyglass unfolded. The lens appeared to be intact. Her spare set of clothes, tied in a neat bundle, were full of sand, but otherwise fine.

She opened the door, hailed the youngster on duty, and requested water. He returned in minutes with a pitcher. Hanna dipped a finger in the vessel. Tepid. Grimacing, she tipped the boy and withdrew into her room.

Hanna wiped her hands on her robe, leaving smears of dirt, sand, and dust on the white fabric, then peeled it off. She quickly shucked her trousers, shirt, and vest; she felt grimy after three days in the desert. Not relishing the lukewarm water, she washed the travel grit off in swift economical movements, rebraided her hair, and pulled on her clothes.

Buckling her hand cannons around her waist, she considered walking out into the Khazad streets with the weapons exposed. The general Khazadian populace wouldn't get too excited about the weapon, since she'd obviously passed the purity inspection at the gate, but it would make her more noteworthy, given the Khazadian fear of such weapons. With a frown creasing her face, she shrugged back into the dirty desert robe.

Hanna looped her satchel across her chest, plopped her hat onto her head, and, patting her vest pockets one last time, strode out of the room.

Now that the sun hung lower in the sky, the streets were nearly impassable as folk took advantage of the cooler temperature. Hanna didn't push or try to hurry. She moseyed along, just one more droplet in the river of people, trusting that eventually she'd get to where she wanted to be.

The spice markets made Hanna's nose itch. So many different scents! Pungent, sweet, sour, savoury—the smells were so vibrant that her mouth watered and her stomach growled. Still allowing the flow of Khazadians, merchants, and tourists to guide her, Hanna browsed several stands, lingering at some, bypassing others, until she reached one with the goods she sought. The reason why she'd accepted the Gelassian job. The little errand that would be a hundred times more profitable than smuggling the Gelassians into the city. Her ticket to retirement.

Saffron. Brilliant yellow saffron stoppered in delicate crystal vials that dangled from wooden racks. The royal purple linen draped over the tables set off the colour of the spice so well that even Hanna blinked, stunned for a moment by the sheer beauty of the display. A faint odor of hay perfumed the air in the tented stand.

Hovering over the racks with the other shoppers, Hanna casually reached into her vest and removed her pocket watch. Using the plump arm of a middle-aged woman as a shield, Hanna flipped open the watch and twisted a fob. The face of the watch unfolded like an accordion, narrowing from the base to the tip. A small lens capped the end. Hanna twisted a second knob, and the tiny camera *clicked-clicked-clicked* as the shutters closed, capturing the image.

"Stop! What are you doing?" A man dressed in saffron-dyed robes peered at her over the heads of several patrons. Muttering in the Khazad tongue, he started pushing through the packed mob.

Hanna pressed a small button and the camera collapsed. She dangled the pocket watch from its chain and spun it in circles. "Just checking the time." She widened her eyes at the merchant who now stood before her, his olive cheeks mottled with red. He grabbed at the watch and Hanna yanked it out of reach.

"No gadgets here! No checking of time." His gaze flickered over her travel-stained robe, and a corner of his mouth curled into a sneer. "Are you buying?"

"I'm looking over your supply, but—"

The merchant snorted. "I see. You are not. You will leave. Do not come back, or I will call for the guards."

The bustle of the tent had quieted. All eyes were on her and the merchant. Shit. Pressing her lips into a smile, Hanna bowed and backed out of the tent. So much for that reconnaissance mission.

Saffron merchants were rare, like the spice, but not impossible to find. In another quarter of an hour, she'd located a second saffron vendor. More tourists milled around in this tent than had been in the first one, so Hanna figured her chances of being unnoticed would be higher.

She was spotted within moments and booted out.

At the sixth saffron booth, she heard mutterings about a snoopy, suspicious-looking foreign woman, and cruised by, stopping at the kebab stand next door. She gulped down pieces of tender, spicy meat, contemplating her string of failures. Hanna had been blessed with pleasant non-descript features: hazel eyes, dirty blonde hair, a nose neither too short nor too long, and thin lips. She could move through a crowd without drawing the least bit of attention. In fact, she had been a successful cutpurse in her youth.

Licking her fingers clean, she narrowed her eyes as a group of familiar figures approached the stand. Passing the purity inspections had worked wonders on the Gelassians, especially their spokeswoman. Her spine had relaxed and she swung her arms as she walked; she was almost slouching.

While the veiled Gelassians ordered their food—Hanna noticed with approval that they ordered vegetable ones, in keeping with the Bezal personas—a drunken customer careened into the stand, knocking a few of the slow-roast spits onto the sand. The Gelassians themselves remained unscathed as, Hanna slowly realized, they had all along.

"Unlucky for other people, not for themselves," she said. She stroked her satchel, picturing the coin bag within. When the Gelassians left the kebab stand, Hanna fell into step beside their spokeswoman.

"Having a nice visit so far?"

The Gelassian jumped. Her large head swivelled in Hanna's direction. "Oh! Mistress − er . . ." Her voice trailed off.

Hanna smiled. "That's right, no names." When the Gelassian spokeswoman would have halted, Hanna stepped in close to her side, the muzzle of her hand cannon pressing into the Gelassian's ribs. "Let's keep walking, shall we? Don't want to draw the wrong kind of attention."

They rejoined the flow of shoppers, two of the Gelassians walking slightly ahead of Hanna and the head female. Hanna's mouth quirked up at one corner as she watched small inconveniences and troubles affect the nearby stalls, but nobody approached the Gelassians. They walked unnoticed, invisible.

"We didn't anticipate crossing paths with you again," the spokeswoman said in a tight voice.

"So I gathered. I noticed a problem with my payment." Hanna shook her satchel. The faint jingle of coins rang just loud enough to be heard over the bustle of the market.

"Oh." The veil twitched as the Gelassian female smiled. "That. Well, we thought—"

"Cut it. To make up for the hassle of exchanging these coins, I'm gonna have to charge you extra."

"Extra! We'll not pay one cent more!"

"Really? You know, the guards here are quite friendly. I noticed that there are rewards for reporting impure beings."

The spokeswoman considered the threat for a few moments, before shrugging in defeat. "We can pay a little more."

Hanna smirked. "Lucky for you, I won't be asking for currency. I need saffron."

"We can't possibly afford saffron!" The Gelassian spokeswoman recoiled from Hanna, hands flapping. "It would be less expensive to double your fee."

"Yeah, but I'm not asking you to *buy* saffron. I'm asking you to *take* it."

The Gelassian female sputtered a few incoherent syllables before squeaking in outrage, "You want us to *steal* for you? Become common criminals?"

Hanna's smirk widened into a grin.

"You do." The Gelassian sighed. "Are you insane? That's against the law!"

"Your being here is against the law. What's a little theft on top of that?"

"A little theft? *Saffron?*" She shook her head. "You are correct, we're already outlaws. However, I cannot make a decision like this without conferring with my companions."

"Sure. I'll give you an hour."

"Very well, Mistress Smuggler. An hour. We will meet you here with our decision."

Hanna drifted away from the Gelassians, her hand lingering on the hand cannon. Gelassians weren't known for violence, but everybody had their breaking point. Hanna figured that the Gelassians had a few viable options, one of which was to physically harm her and continue their vacation in peace. Other possibilities included turning her in for extortion, risking the exposure of their true selves; skedaddling in the next hour (and maybe with them gone Hanna's unlucky streak would end); or accepting her proposition.

Hanna wandered the market, pausing here and there to buy a few trinkets, while she considered everything she knew about Khazad City and its people. Unable to shutter photographs of the saffron tents, and with a disguised Gelassian as an accomplice, she would need a new plan. A faint idea tickled her brain as Hanna meandered back towards the stall where she and the Gelassians had parted company. She prodded at it like a sore tooth while she waited for the Gelassians.

Given the amount of money that they had paid to see Khazad, Hanna would have been surprised if the Gelassians had chosen to flee. Sure enough, two gangly, veiled "Bezal" tourists arrived soon after Hanna. One of them was the spokeswoman with whom Hanna had dealt all along.

Hanna cocked an eyebrow. "The others?"

The female greeted her with a raised palm. "Elsewhere." Her icy tone belied the friendly gesture. "In case this is a trap."

"You wound me with your suspicion," Hanna chuckled, "but I commend your caution. You can't be too careful these days, all sorts of scoundrels wandering around. So, what's the decision?"

The spokeswoman nudged her companion forward. "Weed will help you." She bowed and retreated, allowing herself to be swept away by the crowd.

"Weed? Don't your parents like you?"

"It's not my birth name. It's the name you will call me." Weed shuffled towards her. As tall as the spokeswoman, he didn't have her bearing. The weight of his law-abiding nature had rounded his shoulders and back. "What shall I call you, Mistress Smuggler?"

It was more than a little weird to not see his face. When the troupe had been trekking across the desert, behind her, it hadn't been so bad. Or so necessary. She relied on body language and facial expressions to keep her out of jail, alive, and with a healthy bank account.

"Ondala," she said after a long pause. "You can call me Ondala. So you want to be a thief, huh?"

"I drew the short straw." A hound dog couldn't have had a more mournful tone. He tucked his chin and hunched his shoulders like a tortoise.

"Right." The Gelassians had sent the unluckiest one of their number. It figured. "We'll go over my plan tonight, and hit the spice tents tomorrow."

Weed bowed. "I shall meet you here."

Hanna stepped forward and grabbed his arm. "Oh, no, Junior, you're coming with me." Her free hand drifted down towards her waist.

Weed's head tilted, following the motion. "You wouldn't."

"Try me."

"I told them it wouldn't work." He sighed. "Very well."

"I don't understand why we're taking such a circuitous route," Weed said. His veil flapped in the breeze, and he grabbed the corners, pulling it taut over his face.

Hanna tugged her satchel. The sweet metallic jingle of coins rang in their ears. "I can't carry these into the tent." The city gates and guard towers came into view. Hanna grabbed Weed's sleeve. "Right. Stop here."

The Gelassian halted, and, as his robe billowed about him, Hanna yanked the bag of coins out of her satchel and threw it up in the air. It disappeared over the wall.

Hanna listened for a few minutes, but the guards didn't come rushing out of the towers. She continued strolling. After a few seconds, Weed again fell in step beside her.

Even though Hanna could sense Weed's impatience, she made sure to take a roundabout course to the spice markets. The crowds were thinner this early in the day; more locals, fewer tourists. Their path eventually brought them to the first saffron vendor that Hanna had checked out the previous day. Weed tensed.

"Relax, will you? They'll sense something's up."

"Relax? When we're about," Weed lowered his voice to a dramatic whisper, "*to commit a crime?*"

Hanna shrugged. "If you want to split hairs, I'm committing the crime. You're just . . . window dressing. But," she added, "if I get caught, you're going down with me."

"You keep saying that. We struck a deal, and I'll see it through."

"Right. Sorry." It had only taken a few minutes of conversation the previous night to discover that the Gelassians knew nothing of their jinxing aura. Hanna hoped she could deflect the jinx by saying aloud and often that Weed's fate was tied to hers.

"You don't sound sorry."

Hanna rolled her eyes. "My heartfelt apologies. Now, can we get on with it? The sooner we do it, the sooner you're rid of me. And if all goes well, you'll never see me again."

Weed brushed past her into the saffron vendor's tent. After a count to five hundred, Hanna followed. As they had arranged, Weed stood in the centre of the tent, surrounded by shoppers. Hanna squeezed herself into a spot near the racks of spice vials.

The spice merchant approached her. "I've seen you before, yes? With a gadget? I told you not to—"

A woman screamed. "The Bezal's cloak has torn!"

The few tourists stared in bewilderment as the locals dropped to the ground, shielding their eyes and chanting prayers. Weed fumbled with his clothing, cursing anyone who looked upon his flesh.

Nobody watched Hanna.

It was simple really. The only protection the saffron had was the watchful eyes of the merchant and his employees, all of whom were kneeling on the ground, trembling.

Weed peeked over at her, and, seeing that she had dropped into a crouch and hidden her face, said, "I have repaired my garment. It is safe to open your eyes."

The Khazadians were slow to get up, peering through parted fingers at the disguised Gelassian.

"You!" Someone grabbed the collar of Hanna's desert robe. "Thief!"

Hanna opened her eyes and found herself staring into the

contorted face of the merchant. "Thief?"

"You've stolen my spice!" He waved a hand at the spice racks. Two vials were missing.

"How dare you! I didn't steal anything. Search me, if you'd like."

The merchant didn't release his hold. "Mattias, search this woman."

One of the clerks circled the counter. "Woman, take off your cloak."

Hanna shrugged off the cloak. The spice shoppers went still as her hand cannons came into view. The merchant gulped and gestured for another clerk to come forward. Custody of Hanna safely transferred, the merchant retreated behind the counter, keeping wary eyes on the weapons.

Mattias snatched the cloak up from the ground and squeezed it. Not finding anything, he pulled a small knife from his boot and pointed it at Hanna. "Remove your weapons. Slowly."

Hanna unbelted her hand cannons and lowered them to the ground. Mattias gestured with his knife. "Your bag, give it to me."

Mattias pawed through the satchel like a dog, sniffing Hanna's soiled clothing before tossing it onto the ground. Her spyglass followed with a clank. "Sir!"

The merchant scurried over. Together the two men inspected the bag. The merchant licked his finger, dipped it into the depths of the satchel, and withdrew it. The finger was golden. Gasps whispered around the tent.

"Thief!" the merchant declared.

Hanna snorted and shook her head. "You're nuts."

The merchant smiled. "There is one way to find out." He stuck the finger into his mouth. A curious expression passed over his face, then he coughed, dirty spittle trickling out of his mouth. "Sand. Sand!" He boxed Mattias's ears. "Sand, you idiot!"

Mattias finished the search, but everyone knew that he wouldn't find anything. When he finally shook his head at the spice merchant, more than one onlooker laughed.

"Send for the guards," the merchant said.

Hanna strapped on her hand cannons, then pulled on her desert travel robe. She repacked her satchel while they waited for the guards.

The merchant wasted no time telling them about the missing spice. He pointed at Hanna with a flourish. "I want her removed from the city!"

"Hey! I didn't take your spice, why do I get the boot?"

"I want her gone." The merchant didn't look at her. "She is *bad* for business." He may have well as said "impure", since that was what his tone implied. Several of the locals hissed and forked their fingers at her in the classic sign of the evil eye.

The guards exchanged glances. Moving in unison, they each grabbed one of Hanna's arms. "The saffron merchants are powerful," the one on her right said, not unkindly. "Their every whim is granted."

They lifted her off the ground and strode out of the tent, ignoring her protests. Hanna winked at Weed as she floated past him.

Hanna kept up a steady diatribe as the guards escorted her to the massive city gates. They ignored her, although the tips of their ears turned red. At the gates, they called for the other guards, rather than release her arms. Once the gates opened, they dropped her just outside the city.

"Could I at least have my camel? It's a long trip on foot."

The guards sighed.

"Since my stay has been cut short, the innkeeper owes me some money. You could keep my refund for your troubles," she added, flashing them a sweet smile. Before they could refuse, Hanna gave them the name of the inn.

"Very well," said the one who had spoken before.

Hanna watched them leave, careful not to let a satisfied grin blossom on her face. She walked along the wall, legs folding when she found her bag of Gelassian coins. A swift movement, hidden from the tower guards by her body, transferred the bag to her satchel.

She chuckled. "Good thing I didn't have to shoot my way out of there." Hanna patted her hand cannons, rendered momentarily useless by the slim, crystal vials of saffron stuffed into their muzzles.

She could almost smell the saltwater of Ciscan Bay, and when she closed her eyes, the picture of a house on a cliff filled her mind.

NEITHER SNOW, NOR RAIN, NOR HEAT-RAY

Originally published in *Equus*, edited by Rhonda Parrish. World Weaver Press, 2017.

I was crazy about horses when I was a kid—read about them, drew them, collected toys—so when I came across the call for Equus, *I knew I had to write for it. I don't remember how I hit upon the idea of setting my horse story in* The War of the Worlds *by H.G. Wells, but I love the result.*

NEITHER SNOW, NOR RAIN, NOR HEAT-RAY

London, England, 1900
Five days after the Martian landing

No one had been alarmed when the first Martian vessels had landed, pocking the ground like open sores. They'd only been mildly concerned when the cone-shaped ships vomited forth the spindly, tripod machines. It wasn't until the trains stopped running that panic had set in. Then the tripods had come with their Black Smoke and heat-rays.

Emma swiped the oiled cloth over the bridle again, checking carefully for any cracks in the leather. She would maintain her equipment, as a conscientious and accomplished horse-woman, despite her lacklustre feelings about her assignment. Emma had heard that scientists were working around the clock, designing weapons to combat the Martians and their damnable tripods. In the meantime, the fragmented government and military were organizing an evacuation out of Chelmsford. Most of London had fled the city, Emma's family included, but despite her family's wealth and standing, Emma hadn't been allowed to leave. She'd been—conscripted, she supposed.

A rustle of hay and a velvet nosed pressed against her neck announced the arrival of the reason for her conscription. Emma's death grip on the bridle relaxed and she reached up to stroke the cheek of Beezus, her mare.

The Martians had disrupted communications. Nothing worked, not the telegraph machines nor the new telephones.

Messengers were needed. Messengers on horseback, because human runners were too slow and easily killed by the Martians and their Black Smoke. But horses were scarce so when the general had sighted Beezus, a fine hunter, with a skilled rider—her—they'd been pressed into service on the spot, no matter that she was a girl, a civilian, and a daughter of good family.

And now she and Beezus would be part of the messenger team sent out to the docks—integral to the coordination of the Navy escort for the evacuee ships, or so she'd been told. Emma scowled. Her revolver would've been of better use helping her family travel to Chelmsford than giving messages to a boat.

The mare snorted against her neck and started mouthing her hair. Emma laughed. "Enough of that." She pushed the horse and Beezus obligingly pulled her head back into her stall.

Emma rubbed the mare's nose. "Can't fool you, can I? Yes, we're going out." When Beezus nodded her head, Emma wagged her finger. "Business. Not a pleasure ride."

Beezus huffed.

After checking the mare's water and hay, Emma resumed her equipment check. It was the mare's nervous whinny that halted her. She caught sight of Beezus' wide, rolling eyes and cast a furious glare at the stable door.

"Stay out there!" she yelled. Scowling, she set down the saddle and shut the top half of Beezus' stall door. Maybe that would block the pungent scent of that Moreauvian fiend enough for Beezus to calm down.

Emma opened the stable door, grabbed the arm of the man standing there, and tugged him around the corner of the building toward a garden shed—it wasn't safe for anyone to linger long outside, in case of Martian patrols.

The soldiers had watered down the grounds, washing away most of the deadly Black Smoke, but Emma could see traces of the black grit in the flower beds. She stayed clear of those areas, just in case.

Once inside the shed, she crossed her arms over her chest. "Well?"

He grinned, revealing white, pointed teeth. "Don't you have an office in the barn?"

She sniffed pointedly. "I can't have my barn reeking of

predator. You upset Beezus."

His grin slipped a notch. "They're used to me, up at the house," he offered, chuckling nervously. "Still can't believe they're stabling horses in the ballroom."

"They're preserving my modesty." Emma couldn't help smiling. Here she was, wearing trousers, a revolver belted around her waist, and the general was concerned about her sleeping in the same building as the soldiers.

The Moreauvian pulled a message tube from his pocket and handed it to her. "A map and a copy of your orders."

She took the tube, made no move to empty it. "Thanks." As if the map would be useful, with the polluted landscape and destroyed landmarks.

He seemed to understand. "It has tripod locations marked. Or where they seem to be patrolling, anyhow."

Emma nodded.

He held something else to her. A sweat-stained glove. "You'll need this too." When she hesitated, he clarified, "Your *horse* needs this."

Emma reluctantly accepted the smelly item. Oh, no. She shut her eyes, counted to ten. Re-opening them, she stuffed the glove in her pocket and upended the tube. She scanned the parchment, already knowing what she'd find.

. . . to aid in the successful completion of the mission, several messengers will be sent, following separate routes. They are as follows . . .

She skimmed the list, finding the name she sought at the bottom.

Henry Fletcher, Moreauvian

Bad enough that he was acting as a sort of aide-de-camp. She didn't need the Moreauvian monster on the field in addition to the Martians. Emma rolled up the paper and stuffed it back inside the tube. She did not look at Henry Fletcher.

"All the messengers need an item of clothing, in case we encounter each other—"

"I understand," she snapped. "I have to finish preparing for the ride." When Fletcher didn't move from the door, she said, "Don't you? Have to prepare?"

He shook his head. "I don't need a horse." He paused. "I . . .

can move quite fast . . . when I need to."

She had a good idea of what that meant. Even the lowliest of chimney sweeps had heard of Dr. Moreau and his . . . experiments. She didn't want to hear the details of what Henry Fletcher could do. She gestured to the door. "I have to saddle my horse."

Fletcher sketched a bow and stepped to the side, allowing her to venture out into the gloomy day. "Good luck," he called.

Beezus hated the stink of the glove. She shifted uneasily as Emma fastened the glove to the saddle, moaning.

Emma stroked the mare's shoulder. "He can't smell much worse than a dog, can he?"

Beezus snorted, wagging her head.

"Well, then." Emma whispered into the horse's ear, "I don't like it either, but we'll make do."

Beezus bobbed her head. Emma smiled, resting her forehead against Beezus' neck, breathing deeply of the horse's scent, feeling her heart slow. They would get through this—Black Smoke, Martians, and Moreauvian ally be damned.

Emma inhaled deeply, taking some peace from Beezus' solid presence. She tugged on the bridle's buckles one last time to ensure a secure fit.

Satisfied, she led the mare outside. A small group of soldiers huddled in the yard. There was no sign of Henry Fletcher, or any other messengers. One of the men, the general, approached her.

"You have your orders?" he asked.

Emma nodded. "Yes, sir."

"Right, then." He waved a boy forward, who boosted Emma up on her saddle.

"God speed," the general said and thumped Beezus on the shoulder. "Off you go."

Although the dense Black Smoke eventually sank to the ground, the air was still smoky from decimated buildings and vegetation. People, too, probably. She groped for the message tube containing her orders and the instructions for the fleet and squinted through the haze.

This section of London was desolated, the people long since fled or killed and many of the houses smoking, empty shells. A few, like the one the military had commandeered, were more or less intact. They didn't look inhabited, but then, it wasn't wise to do anything to attract the attention of the tripod patrols. Especially—Emma shuddered—since she'd heard that there were worse fates than death to be had from the tentacles of the Martians.

Going through the city centre would be the quickest route, but the most hazardous—too much rubble obscured by the haze and therefore too risky for Beezus. They would, instead, skirt along the edges of the park and then cut over to the docks. There would be less cover for them, but Beezus was a fine runner. Her speed and nimbleness would get them past the tripods, where human runners and mechanical motors had failed.

It was so quiet that Emma wondered if the Martians had stopped patrolling in this particular area. She guided Beezus around a coach abandoned in the middle of the road. The horses in the harness were dead, sloppily and hastily butchered. Chaos and violence had overcome the people quickly, even in this respectable part of London. Emma grimaced, recalling the confusion yesterday as her family had forced their way through the streets, her father striking people with a riding crop to keep them from climbing atop the laden carriage.

A crash to her left startled her out of her musings. Emma glimpsed a tripod from the corner of her eye and hunched over Beezus' neck, asking the horse for more speed. Their best defence against the tripods was distance. The Black Smoke and heat-rays could not be defeated or deflected, only outrun. Beezus leapt forward as a spindly metal leg stabbed the earth where they'd just been.

Zig-zag, Emma thought, communicating her directions to Beezus through subtle touches of her heels, hands, the reins. The mare responded lightning fast, almost instantaneously. The resounding clangs and stomps of the tripod followed them, not able to catch up despite its long legs, not quite, but—

Zot.

A tree turned to ash on their right as they jigged left.

The heat-ray. Emma's mouth went dry. Probably better than

canisters of Black Smoke, but still not good.

Zot.

Emma stood up in her stirrups, her head alongside Beezus' neck. She was calm. There was her, there was Beezus, and there was the road in front of them. The buzzing of heat-rays was no more bothersome than a fly.

"Cart!" she yelled. Beezus' ear flicked, but she'd already seen the obstacle. Her muscles bunched, and Emma adjusted her seat as the horse jumped the over-turned cart.

Beezus came down fine, no stumbles, and Emma was already communicating a course direction as the cart disintegrated behind them.

Emma glanced over her shoulder. The tripod didn't seem to be gaining. Would it let them escape? Find easier prey, or—

Emma steered Beezus off the road into the trees as a second tripod erupted from the houses, a heat-ray blasting holes in the road.

Emma gulped. They'd have to slow down, sacrificing speed for the cover of trees. Beezus pushed through a clump of bushes and Emma nearly sobbed with relief as the mare's hooves came down on a well-maintained bridle path. Beezus picked up her pace, her stride lengthening, and the noise of the tripods faded.

These trees here were faring well, still leafy and green—healthy—and with none of the powdery residue of the Black Smoke. It was tempting to stop, to rest, but she didn't dare. What if the tripods decided to follow her into the park? Distance. Distance was her best defence.

Gradually, the trees thinned and then ended abruptly, abutting against a once-elegant house which now lay in ruins. Smoke spiralled in the distance. Through the miasma, Emma could see dark, irregular shapes. Houses, perhaps, with their roofs blown away.

Beezus shifted and whickered softly. Emma patted her neck. "Hush, my lovely. Let's get our bearings."

Emma pulled out the map. Buildings would be next to useless, but surely the park . . . ? She located it on the map and grunted with surprise. They had come farther than she'd thought. The road before them would lead to the docks—the Navy. If they were even there.

These ships, she had heard, had been called from the North by telegraph before the Martians had disrupted communications. They might not have arrived yet. And if they had, they might have been discovered by the tripods and burnt to ash with the heat-rays, or the crews killed with the Black Smoke.

She sighed, staring glumly at the road. The surest way to reach her destination; the surest way to be found by tripods. She peeked behind her. The park was silent and green. No Black Smoke, no rotting corpses, no foulness. She and Beezus could scrabble there for a while. The Navy and the Army could fight the Martians, figure out ways to counteract the Black Smoke and heat-rays. It was *their* responsibility, *their* duty. She and Beezus would sit this out. They would be safe.

But her father was on the road to Chelmsford, along with hundreds, maybe thousands of people. The Navy needed to be there to guard the retreat and to do that they needed to be told where to go. She stroked the butt of her revolver. She couldn't be with her family, but she could still ensure that they escaped the Martians.

Emma patted the mare and urged her forward. "We'll see it through to the end."

Beezus' eager strides ate the road, and it wasn't long before the odor of the Thames reached them. Sewage. Fish. Rotting humans.

Many of the buildings were husks, the air full of smoke and dust and grit, the hazy sky making it difficult to gauge the distance to the actual docks. Bodies littered the streets and sidewalks, trampled, rather than victims of the Black Smoke. She didn't want to imagine the horror and chaos of yesterday's evacuation. A glimmer of white shone through the haze and her heart jumped in her chest. Sails!

As she directed Beezus toward the sails, a dark form darted into the street in front of them. Emma blinked. Another rider? She whooped with excitement. Another rider had survived the journey!

The second rider also veered toward the glimmer of sails. Emma bent low over Beezus' neck. They would arrive together, triumphant, and see the ships off to Chelmsford where the evacuees waited.

Flooded with elation, Emma nearly missed the tremor that

shook the earth.

Beezus didn't.

The mare canted sharply to the left. The ground burst behind them, spewing rocks and dirt. A Black Smoke canister? Emma kept her mouth shut tight and prayed for Beezus to run faster.

Peeking underneath her arm, Emma could see the low-hanging cloud of Black Smoke. And beyond that, the tripod navigating the narrow streets between buildings. She gulped. It was stepping *over* the buildings. But it had to sacrifice speed for the shortcut, since it could only move one spindly leg at a time, ensuring solid footing before initiating its next step.

Emma turned forward. Beezus could outrun it and the Black Smoke, she was positive. But . . . with a tripod so close, they wouldn't be able to watch the ship take sail. In fact . . . in fact, they would have to charge the tripod after delivering the message. She and Beezus playing decoy while the ship made way.

Emma gulped again, laying one hand flat against the mare's neck. They would do it. They wouldn't—couldn't—falter now, not with so many relying on them.

Maybe, she thought, and the tightness eased in her throat, maybe with the other rider, she and Beezus could peel away now, lead that monstrous machine a merry chase in the park, and give everyone a better chance at survival.

Her fingers tensed on the reins, and Beezus' ears twitched, waiting for the new direction.

Zot.

A hole, in front of them.

Zot.

A building, engulfed in flames, spewing ash.

A rock struck Beezus and she squealed, weaving sideways.

"Don't fall, don't fall, don't fall," Emma chanted, hauling on the reins to help the mare recover her balance.

Beezus' stride smoothed, and Emma drew her to a halt.

"We're lucky its aim is so bad," she panted, slapping the mare's shoulder and leaning to one side to check for a wound.

Zot.

A horse screamed.

Emma jerked upright and gasped. The other messenger was . . . gone. His horse—

Gagging, Emma drew her revolver and fired. The terrible shrieking ceased, and Emma dug her heels into Beezus' side. Beezus bolted forward, and Emma holstered her weapon before concentrating on guiding Beezus through the debris- and corpse-ridden street. They could still make the ship, a promise of hope gleaming in the grey, smoky air.

A second tripod appeared among the buildings and strode down the street toward them.

"*Damn* it!" Emma yelled.

The shock froze her brain for a moment, but the sails beckoned. They could dash behind that abandoned carriage, dodge into the alleys . . . use the buildings as shields. The alleys probably connected and formed their own crooked and narrow pathway to the docks. Before she could put the sketchy plan into action, Beezus neighed and rushed straight for the Martian tripod.

"No!" Emma yanked on the reins. "Beezus, no!"

Red light blazed on the hull of the tripod. Emma shut her eyes.

Zot.

Squealing . . . metal?

Emma's eyes snapped open. Beezus was still running like hell for the new tripod. Emma threw a glance over her shoulder. A hole smouldered in the body of the first tripod; its legs wobbled. With another scream of distressed metal it toppled, crashing to the earth with a resounding thud.

Tingly with shock, Emma looked again to the new tripod, the one which had destroyed its comrade.

"Beezus, how did you—?"

A portion of the tripod slid open. A human, not a tentacled Martian, popped into view.

"Make for the ship! Hurry, before another of the damned things arrive!"

Emma squinted. "Fletcher? Henry Fletcher?"

The Moreauvian messenger waved. "I'll keep watch!" he shouted. "Hurry!" He ducked into the machine and the door slid shut.

With no further obstacles, Beezus ran between the spindly legs of their unlikely saviour, Emma too stunned to do anything but provide basic guidance.

Emma watched the ship make way, tears streaming down her face. With luck, *Thunder Child* would rendezvous with the evacuation fleet.

She leaned against her mare's shoulder. "Sorry for doubting you, my lovely," she murmured. "I won't do that again."

Beezus snorted and bobbed her head.

"That was some riding," said Henry Fletcher, stepping up beside her.

Emma wrinkled her nose at his musky scent and laughed. "I just hung on. She did all the hard work." She hesitated. "Listen, Fletcher, I'm sorry for being so rude earlier. Thank you for saving us. For saving Beezus." She proffered a hand.

He gripped it and gave it a firm shake, and she noticed for the first time that his fingers were tipped with thick, pointed claws.

"Think no more of it," he said.

Emma smiled. "We're returning to headquarters now. Will you—will you accompany us?"

Fletcher looked surprised and his cheeks reddened. "I would be honoured to, under ordinary circumstances, but I have a feeling our Navy will need some help with the evacuees. And I can provide formidable support."

"Oh, of course," she said, squashing a surge of disappointment. "That's a brilliant plan. I'll inform the general." Impulsively, she kissed his cheek. "Good luck, Fletcher."

"And to you," he said. "Farewell, Beezus." He stroked the mare's forehead, bowed to Emma, and hurried to his tripod.

Emma watched as he scaled the tripod legs with, she presumed, his claws and clambered into the body. Once it had stalked off and she could no longer see it, she grabbed Beezus' bridle.

"We've a ways to go before we can rest, my lovely," she said, guiding Beezus toward the park.

She had to report to the general. What she'd seen and done today would prove valuable for the military and the scientists. Aiding the evacuees was just the first step, she realized. The next step would be eradicating the Martian invaders. Messengers would be needed.

She and Beezus would be needed.

It was their duty.

THE ADVENTURE OF THE PALE DEATH

Originally published in *Sherlock Holmes: Further Adventures in the Realms of H.G. Wells, Volume One*, edited by Derrick Belanger. Belanger Books, 2021.

In addition to speculative fiction, I adore mysteries. But my sweet spot involves mashing those two genres together. "The Adventure of the Pale Death" stars Sherlock Holmes and Dr. Watson, solving crime in the aftermath of the Martian invasion from The War of the Worlds *by H.G. Wells.*

THE ADVENTURE OF THE PALE DEATH

I t was a grim ride through the city to Parliament Hill. Black
sludge, the remnants of the black smoke fired by the Martian
tripods, coated the ground. Some intrepid souls attempted to
clear the streets, taking care not to touch the foul substance. It
was a sensible precaution—no one knew if the toxic elements
were inert in the smoke's solid form.

Sherlock Holmes sucked on a pipe, and while he faced the
streets, I wasn't entirely sure he saw them.

Holmes stirred and glanced at me. The past several days had
exacted a toll on him, the skin over his cheekbones pulled taut
and dark circles rimmed his eyes.

"Quite the puzzler my brother gave us, eh, Watson?" he asked,
knocking ash from his pipe against the cart.

"You read my mind, Holmes," I said.

Holmes's thin lips quirked into a brief smile. "Nonsense,
Watson, it's a logical subject to occupy one's mind. My brother
shows up in Mrs. Hudson's cellar and sends us off on a mission
to Parliament Hill, as if . . ."

Holmes at a lack of words was an unusual condition. I
hastened to fill the space. "As if there could be anything more
important than recovering from the invasion?"

"Just so, Watson," he said.

The wagon jolted, and I was knocked against the sides as the driver cursed and then praised his carthorse. Most conveyances had been hired for the flight from London, and it had taken some time to track down this hostler. The carthorse was a bony nag, and it was a wonder it was able to pull the cart at all.

Holmes had resumed what I would call nervous puffing in any other man. I would do the same, I'm sure, if I had a cigar. As it was, my fingers clutched the handle of my medical bag so tightly that my knuckles were white. The panic and dread of the invasion tainted Mycroft Holmes's assignment.

Mycroft had appeared that morning impeccably dressed, an incongruous sight in Mrs. Hudson's cellar, which we had converted to a shelter for people hiding from the Martian tripod patrols. Holmes and I were in shirtsleeves, smeared with soot and grime and blood.

Mycroft had surveyed our refuge in silence for a few moments before striding over to Holmes. His experience was needed, Mycroft explained. A possible threat to the kingdom.

He'd given no further details, not wanting to prejudice Holmes's perceptions. Holmes's eyebrows had arched at that, and although I recognized the peevish glint in his eyes, he had agreed to assist Mycroft.

"Watson," Holmes called softly, startling me out of my reverie.

I became aware that the jouncing motion of the cart had ceased and yelped when I took note of our surroundings.

"Hideous contraption, isn't it?" Holmes said, almost cheerfully, as he hopped out of the wagon. I clambered out more slowly, eyes not leaving the monstrous tripod that dominated Parliament Hill.

Men were climbing the tripod—science researchers, I presumed, or perhaps engineers. On the ground before the spindly legs, a large tarp covered a misshapen lump. A Martian?

Parliament Hill had been scarred by the Martians. Their flying ship cylinder had plowed through the turf, and in the furrow created by the ship, they had erected numerous odd machines. And there was the pit, of course.

I'd heard rumours of the pits, but had hoped it was just nightmare speculation. But judging from the unpleasant odor wafting form the pit, all the stories were true.

It was here, I was certain, that Mycroft wished us to

concentrate our efforts. Holmes was no engineer, and there were already several people exploring the many Martian machines.

Holmes had already reached that conclusion, for he was striding towards the pit, a handkerchief held over his face. Drawing out my own handkerchief, I followed.

Up close, the handkerchief did little to mask the stench of the pit. Holmes had returned his to his pocket. He stared into the hole sombrely. I couldn't determine how many bodies were in the pit, but they were pale and mutilated—victims of the Martians' appetites. It looked as if they had been punctured, and I would theorize that the extreme pallor was a result of blood loss.

I wanted to tear my eyes away, but didn't. I forced myself to examine the corpses, acknowledging the many, many puncture wounds—

"Holmes!" I cried.

"I see it as well, Watson. Can you come down?"

Holmes was already descending, step-sliding down the slope of the pit. I hurried after him.

The anomaly was a deceased male. An albino, with only one visible wound: a hole in his head.

Fortunately, he lay close to the edge of the pit, so that we were not forced to walk upon the macabre carpet of the pits' contents.

Holmes squatted and peered intently at the body. With deft motions, he checked the deceased's fingers and hands and prodded gently at the fatal wound.

"This man wasn't a victim of the Martians," he said. "But someone hoped he would be taken for one."

"That's a gunshot wound," I said.

"I concur, Watson." Holmes looked up towards the tripod. "I wonder if a few of those lads would help us bring this poor old fellow up out of here. I'll need to perform a more thorough search of his person."

The men didn't want to work with a dead body, but a combination of money and an appeal to their better natures did the trick.

Holmes went through the man's pockets, inspected the shirt cuffs, his shoes, the hems of his trousers. He pulled a black hair from the man's coat. He stared at it thoughtfully, then wrapped it in a piece of paper which he stuck into an inner pocket of his coat.

"Watson," he said, finally, standing up. "I believe the gunshot wound is the cause of death, but I will defer to your expert opinion, if you would be so kind."

As I knelt beside the poor soul, Holmes withdrew a notebook from the side pocket of his coat. Holmes possessed enough artistic skill to render a likeness of our mysterious victim, although the most distinguishing feature, the albinism, could not be portrayed with a pencil.

"As you surmise, Holmes, the gunshot wound is the likely cause," I reported. "Of course, it's possible he ingested something, but I can't ascertain anything like that under these circumstances." I slowly climbed to my feet, cursing my stiff leg. "There are some odd stains on his hands."

"Ah! I wondered if that would catch your attention, Watson. Our man here was a science researcher. Those are chemical stains."

"Science researcher?" I repeated.

"There are other indications which I've made note of, but I won't bore you with the details."

"With the city in such chaos, it will be difficult to find a missing researcher, Holmes, even an albino one. There are too many missing persons just now."

"We have one clue in that regard, Watson: Mycroft's interest. That should narrow the field somewhat."

"It would have been easier if Mycroft had just directed us to this man's laboratory—he obviously knows who he is," I grumbled.

Holmes chuckled. "My brother no doubt wished to pique my interest—which it is—whereas ordering me about like an automaton would have irritated me and worked against his interests. Furthermore, seeing the body in situ is always useful. So many clues."

He clapped my shoulder. "Come, Watson. We'll head to the government laboratory, after we make transport arrangements for our friend here."

I had never been clear about which branch of the government Mycroft worked for—or led (he wasn't clear about that either).

But what was clear was that it ranked in the upper echelons of the government and wielded a great deal of power and influence.

Why then the building which housed their operations resembled a grey cube, I couldn't guess. It was also untouched by the Martian invasion, which was something of a miracle, based on the debris surrounding it. Part of the terror of the Martian invasion was the randomness of their destructive plans.

Holmes paid the cart driver generously for the trip and promised more if he waited for us. The aged driver grunted and tipped his cap. Interpreting that as agreement, Holmes and I left the driver and proceeded into the building.

It was very quiet, and no one staffed the receptionist desk. Holmes had just started rifling through drawers when someone demanded, "Who are you? What are you doing there?"

The speaker was a young man in a white lab coat, which was dotted with odd stains. His eyes were bloodshot and a little crazed, and his black hair was unkempt. I silently diagnosed exhaustion.

Holmes introduced himself, adding, "I'm here on Her Majesty's business, along with—"

"Oh, Dr. Moreau isn't going to be happy," said the man.

Holmes frowned. "We're looking for this man and have reason to believe he works here." Holmes withdrew the notebook and opened it, holding it up for the man to see. "He's also an albino."

The young man's suspicious scowl relaxed and he sighed. "Oh, for God's sake, what has Griffin done now? You found him passed out in a gutter, I suppose?"

"Griffin?" Holmes repeated.

The young science researcher shrugged, lips pooching in a sullen smirk. "*Dr.* Griffin, technically. The star of Dr. Moreau's lab. He's working on—" he broke off, looking guilty. He probably wasn't allowed to divulge the projects in the laboratory.

"We need to speak with Dr. Griffin's laboratory team or his supervisor—whomever he reports to," Holmes said.

"Well, I suppose . . . has he been arrested?" the man asked. "Dr. Moreau can vouch for his character. Griffin's work is too important for him to languish in a gaol cell with the drunks."

"Thomson, what the devil is taking so long, boy?" boomed another voice.

The new arrival was a large middled-aged man with somewhat coarse features. A thick mop of stark white hair capped his head, contrasting sharply with his bright black eyes, which were shadowed by bushy eyebrows. He also wore a laboratory coat. While the stains on young Thomson's coat were unidentifiable, the stains on this man's coat were unmistakably from blood.

"Oh, hullo," he said, noticing us. Then, dismissing us, he turned to the younger man. "Go fetch the files from my office, Thomson, there's a good lad."

Thomson hunched his shoulders. "I was just showing these men—"

"Above your pay grade, lad," said the older man. The words were kind, but the tone was hard. "You're holding up my work. I don't need another screw-up from you today." Thomson blanched and scurried away.

"I'm Sherlock Holmes," Holmes said quietly. "And I'm here about your man Griffin."

"Griffin?" He considered Holmes for a moment, and I thought he meant to dismiss us again. Holmes must have thought that, too, as his gaze sharpened and his lean frame tensed, a hound waiting for the hunt signal.

"I'm Moreau," the man said. "Leading the research department of which Griffin was a member. Talented researcher. Nervy, though. High strung, like a blue-blooded horse." He paused again, then added thoughtfully, "Drinks too much. Fights with everyone."

He cast Holmes a piercing glare and demanded, "So, what about Griffin, then? You'll be recompensed for any damage he's done, and please send our apologies to whatever poor sod he's punched this time. Talented man like that, bound to let off some steam now and then, you understand—Holmes, you said your name was?"

"Yes," Holmes said icily. "As for your man Griffin, I'm afraid I've bad news. He's dead."

"Dead?" Moreau's face slackened with shock.

"Dead," Holmes confirmed. "I am here on an official inquiry into his death, and as such, I'll need access to his laboratory space."

Moreau sputtered, his face flushing. "Impossible! Top secret, our work, and not to be viewed by civilians. Just because a man dies, doesn't give you the right to disrupt my work!"

"I didn't make myself clear," Holmes said, and there was no mistaking the pleasure in his voice. "Griffin was murdered. That does trump the importance of your work and grants me access to his workspace." He smiled coldly. "Now."

After more blustering, Moreau led us to his basement laboratory. Holmes impatiently strode behind Moreau, but not so impatiently that he did not take in his surroundings. Not that there was much to see. The walls were a sterile grey. At irregular intervals, uncomfortable-looking benches squatted in the corridors. The interior of the building was as bland as the exterior.

Finally, Moreau came to a halt. "Here it is," he said and then closed his mouth with an audible click, as if cutting off more words.

Holmes gestured for him to proceed, and Moreau complied, a fierce frown beetling his brow.

The laboratory hummed with activity, a shocking sight after the unnatural hush of the rest of the building. Animal cages lined one wall, while along a second were tables laden with beakers and scientific equipment that were unknown to me. A couple of medical gurneys were stuffed into a corner. There were at least a half dozen people working at various tables or desks.

As we entered, a woman rushed to Dr. Moreau. Her thick black hair was arranged in a bun high on her head, although several thick tendrils had escaped and curled to her shoulders. Her eyes, a curious green-yellow shade, flicked to us before she focused on Moreau. "Doctor, I believe we've had a breakthrough with—"

"Forgive me, my dear, but that will have to wait," Moreau said. He glanced at Holmes, looked back at the woman, and said, "There's been a tragedy. Griffin is dead—murdered! And this gentleman, Sherlock Holmes, is making inquiries into the matter."

She gasped. "Murdered! But how? They're all—" She stopped. Moreau had grabbed her arm and now released it, chuckling.

"Now, now, Catherine," he murmured. "No need to tell these

gentlemen everything. Mr. Holmes would like to see Griffin's workspace and ask a few questions. Can you see to that, my dear?" At her nod, he smiled pleasantly, although his eyes remained dark and unreadable. "Catherine—Miss Hardwick—is my assistant and can help you with your inquiries. I'll be in my office should you need me."

I murmured a thanks, and Moreau's dark gaze settled on me. "I didn't catch your name . . . ?"

"Hudson," Holmes interjected smoothly. "Mr. Hudson is *my* assistant. Takes all my notes."

I opened my mouth, and Holmes's foot trod forcefully on my toes, so what came out of my mouth was, "I'll need to stay by Mr. Holmes's side, to take good quality notes," instead of a sputtering protest of being so grossly mistreated.

The pressure on my foot eased, and I belatedly realized that Holmes didn't want Moreau to know my true qualifications, and thus, I couldn't be presented as John Watson. My name did occasionally appear alongside Holmes's in the newspapers, and, of course, I enjoyed a slight fame as the chronicler of Holmes's cases.

Moreau and his assistant, Miss Hardwick, didn't seem to notice anything strange about my reply. Moreau gave a little bow and left, while Miss Hardwick regarded us apprehensively.

"Griffin's workspace?" Holmes prompted.

"Yes, of course." She turned on her heels, and Holmes and I quickly followed.

"I hope my notes meet expectations," I muttered.

"Keep your eyes open, my dear Hudson," Holmes replied, his tone so mild that I shot him a glance. He was smiling, to my annoyance, but his eyes were directed ahead, past Miss Hardwick to the table that sat beyond her. I put aside my irritation and reminded myself that Holmes often utilized disguises and aliases in his investigations. It was just my turn for such a necessary deception.

"Optics?" Holmes asked, stepping to Miss Hardwick's side in front of the table. Deftly, he plucked a black strand of hair from her shoulder.

Several prisms and mirrors stood along the length of the table, plus beakers and extensive tubing. An odd cylindrical device dominated one end of the workspace.

"Yes, Griffin was experimenting with refraction," Miss Hardwick said.

I couldn't make heads nor tails of the ensuing questions which Holmes posed to Miss Hardwick, let alone Miss Hardwick's answers. My attention and gaze wandered and eventually, both were caught by the animal cages. Cats, dogs, a chimpanzee, scores of rats, even some lambs. What did animals have to do with optics experiments? I wondered.

I turned to Holmes, who was watching me while uttering polite responses to Miss Hardwick's recitation of refraction indexes. Holmes tilted his head at the animals. I raised my eyebrows and he inclined his head in an infinitesimal nod. Then, he shifted position to block Miss Hardwick's immediate view of me.

Emboldened, I walked to the cages. The other science researchers were almost aggressively indifferent to my actions, and I wondered what kind of leader Moreau was, to inspire such blind obedience. I recalled Thomson's fright earlier and concluded that Moreau wasn't someone I'd want to work for or with.

The animals were rather pitiful. Dull eyes, poor coat condition, listless dispositions—they were undernourished. I frowned. Being a medical doctor, I understood all too well the necessity of using animals for experiments, but needless cruelty such as neglect and starvation was ill-becoming.

A small white cat mewed piteously, and I smiled at her. "There's a good puss," I said, and reached in to pet her. To my consternation, the cat faded from sight! My fingers, though, distinctly felt fur beneath their tips, and my stomach roiled uncertainly. What kind of optical illusion was this? A cat where there was no cat?

Optical illusion? I threw a startled glance at Griffin's workspace. There were chemicals on the table. What was their purpose, I wondered.

The space under my hands shimmered, and I could once again see the cat. Her milky white fur shone like the moon and flickered in and out of my vision.

I yanked my hand back, and the cat gave a reproachful *miaow*.

The chimpanzee grunted in reply, and I looked towards it.

My brain froze, every part of me so completely repelled that I couldn't even make a sound. The chimpanzee stared at me mournfully, then raised its human hand to scratch its nose. I leant closer and examined it. Yes, the hand was human. The creature was not. How was such a thing possible?

"What are you doing over here? Doctor Moreau said you were to stay with Miss Hardwick and the detective."

A rail-thin blond man glared at me, lips pursed in disapproval.

"I . . . uh . . . Mr. Holmes needs me."

I stumbled away from the blond man and the cages with their horrible contents and returned to Holmes's side.

"Holmes," I hissed, "this place is a house of horrors!"

"Indeed," Holmes said, "have you looked closely at our guide?"

Miss Hardwick was in the process of setting up an experiment with Griffin's equipment. I stared at her. Lithe and graceful, she manoeuvred the equipment with familiarity and ease. Recalling the chimpanzee, I gave special attention to her hands. Or rather, her paws, because while the fingers were elongated and furless, the claws protruding from her fingertips weren't human. They were feline.

"At least she's visible," I quietly said.

"Visible, Hudson?" Holmes rubbed his chin. "Then it is Griffin."

He offered no explanation for that strange remark. There wasn't any doubt that Griffin was dead. Was there?

"Listen, Hudson," Holmes said, "don't say anything about the animals' peculiarities, understand?"

"But, Holmes—"

"Not a word!"

I nodded, not bothering to hide my displeasure.

"You never answered my question, Mr. Hudson."

I groaned. The blond researcher had followed me, and he had brought the other researchers with him. They fanned out behind him, an effective wall between us and the exit. Silent and glowering at me, the researchers were now a forbidding bunch, large and hulking. And did that one have tusks? No, that, I was sure, was my imagination.

"Er," I stammered.

"You were to stay with Catherine," the blond man said. "Catherine, how could you let this man roam around the lab?"

Miss Hardwick shrank into herself. "I didn't know, Montgomery. I was helping Mr. Holmes, as instructed. He wanted to see the refraction experiment." The last few words poured out in a torrent, barely intelligible.

"Miss Hardwick was quite helpful," Holmes said. His voice was calm and his body loose, but he stood on the balls of his feet—ready for action.

Montgomery and the other researchers stepped forward, and my hand strayed to my pocket. I seldom ventured on a case with Holmes without my service revolver, and that was doubly true when Mycroft was involved.

"What's the meaning of this?" Moreau shouted. Young Thomson trailed him through the room to join the wall of researchers. "Montgomery, have you lost your wits?"

Montgomery's fists unclenched. "No, Dr. Moreau." He pointed at me. "This man was at the cages."

"Oh?" Moreau smiled, but it contained no cheer. "And what did you think of our animals, Mr. Hudson?"

Holmes had warned me not to speak about the animals' peculiarities, and I suddenly realized the real danger we were in. I wasn't an accomplished liar, to Holmes's vexation and amusement, but there was a way to be truthful without endangering Holmes or me.

"There's a cat with a shimmering coat," I said. "At times it was like she wasn't there at all. Invisible. Is that what Griffin was working on?" My mind made a sudden leap. "Miss Hardwick was explaining refraction to Mr. Holmes."

Everyone relaxed. First Moreau, then Montgomery, Thomson, and the other researchers, and then finally, Holmes.

"Well done, Hudson," he murmured.

"Yes, invisibility," Moreau said. "Our government is quite keen about his research. No doubt they're distressed about his death."

Holmes hummed an agreement. "Some military applications, I believe."

"Yes." Moreau waved a hand dismissively.

"I've seen what I needed," Holmes said. "I am sorry to disrupt your work, but your researcher Thomson will need to leave with us."

Moreau blinked.

"He killed Griffin here last night," Holmes continued, "and tried to hide his deed in a Martian death pit. Mr. Hudson and I will escort him to the Yard."

Thomson whimpered and took a shambling step backwards.

"The motive," Holmes said, words dropping like stones, "is still unclear. Jealousy over lab hierarchy? Possible, but Griffin's work, though connected, seems mostly separate from yours, Dr. Moreau." Holmes pressed his palms together and tapped the steepled fingers against his mouth. "Personal vendetta? Somehow, monetary gain seems unlikely."

All eyes were fixed on Thomson. He took another step towards the exit.

"Do share, Thomson. Did Griffin yell at you? Call you names? Did you *screw up?*"

Thomson flinched and stumbled. "I couldn't—I couldn't advance in Moreau's group, there's too many of us. I thought . . . I thought I could help with the optics, but he laughed at me. He laughed! Said I was too pedestrian!" Thomson's voice cracked.

"So you shot him?" Holmes prodded.

"Yes, yes, I shot him!" Thomson howled, collapsing to the floor.

"We keep guns in the lab, in case the dogs escape," Moreau commented, staring at Thomson like he was an interesting splotch under a microscope.

"He was right!" Thomson screeched. "I can't read his notes. They're written in gibberish!"

"Probably code," Holmes remarked quietly to me. "Where are the notes, Thomson? Where are Griffin's notes?"

But Thomson refused to answer. Not then, not in the interminable ride back to Scotland Yard, and not to any officials, government or otherwise. Despite his capital offense, Thomson was not hanged, in the hope that one day he would disclose the location of Griffin's notes—for repeated searches of Thomson's lab, home, and favourite haunts yielded nothing.

"He probably destroyed them," I said a few days later.

Some areas of our quarters at 221B were still intact after the Martian invasion. Mrs. Hudson was looking to hire contractors to rebuild the damaged portions, but as the entire city was trying to hire builders, she hadn't any success yet.

Luckily, Holmes's sitting room was more or less untouched. The windows were unbroken and none of the Black Smoke had breached the room.

"No, I don't believe so," Holmes said. "He would have bragged about it."

I prepared to ask another question but was interrupted by a perfunctory knock and then the opening of the door. Mycroft Holmes filled the doorway: tall, large, and dapper. He removed his hat as he crossed the threshold, cane *thunk*ing with authority against our carpet.

"Well, Sherlock, my thanks to you," he said primly, settling into an armchair across from Holmes. "Although I'd hoped you'd recover Griffin's notes. None of those twits in Moreau's laboratory can explain how the contraption works."

I thought of Miss Hardwick and shifted in my seat. Holmes caught my eyes, and although he didn't say a word, something in his gaze stilled my tongue.

"Yes, Watson?" Mycroft asked, fixing his hawk eyes on me.

"I understood Griffin to be a difficult personality, and none of the others liked to be in his company," I said honestly.

Holmes smiled faintly.

"Indeed," Mycroft said. He turned back to his brother. "So, the Griffin affair remains half resolved. What of the other, Sherlock?"

The other? I, too, turned to Holmes.

Holmes slouched further in his chair, legs stretched far in front of him. "Moreau? Cut him loose, Mycroft. His vivisection experiments are unconscionable. They'll reflect poorly on Her Majesty."

Mycroft sighed. "I feared that was the case."

"He should be more than cut loose!" I exclaimed. "His medical license should be revoked."

I was again pinned by Mycroft's intense gaze. "I'll take that under advisement, Dr. Watson. Perhaps we'll run him out of the country, too." He set the cane firmly against the floor and stood. "Her Majesty appreciates your service, Sherlock, especially in these tumultuous times. I've left the name of a building company with Mrs. Hudson. I'm sure she'll find their rates to be more than reasonable."

He walked to the exit, pausing in the doorway to put on his hat. "Oh, and Sherlock? Do let me know if you find those plans, will you?" He gently shut the door behind him.

"Why does Mycroft think you'll find those plans? And why couldn't I talk about Miss Hardwick? She could help them figure out Griffin's experiment."

Holmes regarded me through heavy-lidded eyes. "Miss Hardwick doesn't deserve to be shackled to our military. Her situation will be awkward enough with the imminent public flogging of Dr. Moreau."

"Yes, but, Holmes—"

"I've heard that a troupe without a theatre will be giving a performance in the park, Watson. Fancy a play?"

I nodded, even as I gaped at him. Holmes knew where the plans were. But as my stolid mind explored the possibilities of Griffin's experiment, I decided that Holmes was right to not disclose their location to Mycroft. We were surrounded by a ruined, devastated city. We didn't need Griffin's experiment with military applications. We'd seen enough of war.

"A play would be an enjoyable distraction, Holmes," I said.

THE ADVENTURE OF THE BELL DEVICE

Originally published as "The Adventure of the Crab Bisque" in *Brave New Girls: Tales of Girls who Tech and Tinker*, edited by Paige Daniels and Mary Fan. Brave New Girls, 2020.

The second story in the Carrie Wheelwright series features even more steampunk gadgets and even more spy adventures for the teenager.

THE ADUENTURE OF THE BELL DEUICE

Vancouver, British Columbia
1891

S etting up the spy devices in the dining room was taking longer than planned. The grandfather clock ticked ominously as Carrie Wheelwright crawled under the massive table, affixing the hastily constructed gadgets.

Her best friend, Maria Acevado, suddenly popped into view, and Carrie gave a startled shout.

"Sorry." Maria grinned. "I just finished placing all the devices along the sideboards. How're you doing?"

"This table is huge," Carrie hissed. "Only two left." She crawled a few more paces, blowing her unruly hair out of her face, and stopped when she reached a brace. Tucking the pronged, cylindrical device, which resembled the inner workings of a player piano, between bolts, Carrie fastened it into place with some adhesive.

Perhaps it would have been better to plant her spy gadgets in the centrepieces, but she was worried they would be discovered. Gentlemen, she supposed, wouldn't spend much time gazing at flowers, but women might, and there were an equal number of women as men invited to the embassy dinner.

Carrie stuck the last one to the table with a grunt, then crawled out from under the table.

"Will they work?" Maria asked.

Carrie nodded, but then sighed and shrugged. "I think so. But we haven't had time to properly test them, and retrieving information from them might be difficult. While Alexander Graham Bell has made marvellous progress with auditory—"

"Probably, then," Maria interrupted. "Great. And if they fail, it's your sister's fault."

Carrie winced. Louisa. Carrie hadn't seen much of her sister since the debacle last year. After nearly ruining the family's reputation and prospects by conspiring with Russian agents, Louisa had eloped with an American diplomat, one Joseph Dalton. The scandal had haunted the society pages of the newspaper for weeks.

Today, Louisa had sent a telegram to Carrie, inviting her to tea. Carrie had accepted, hoping for a reconciliation with her sister—Mother and Father were wan shadows of their usual robust selves and a shroud of melancholy hung over the Wheelwright household. Anticipating a certain amount of awkwardness, Carrie had brought Maria for emotional support.

However, instead of sandwiches and apologies, Carrie had found herself roped into Louisa's latest scheme: eavesdropping on the dinner guests of the American embassy. Carrie had been sorely tempted to refuse, but the idea of Louisa owing Carrie a favour was appealing. After a whispered consultation with Maria, the two girls had agreed to help. Commandeering a cold and seldom-used study, Carrie had built several listening devices, improvising wildly from Bell's work with gramophones. At Louisa's direction, the devices were planted all over the dining room. Not only to catch stray conversation during dinner, but also the men's after-dinner conversation, when the women left the room.

"She should've questioned her sources again. Or found new ones," Maria grumbled as she and Carrie packed up their tools.

"Not enough time," Carrie said. "The maid Louisa overheard never came back to work after that day, and the plot will take place this week—Louisa searched for her, but hasn't had any luck."

"She left the city," Maria said.

"I hope so," Carrie replied. The alternative was too horrible to contemplate. Maria nodded with understanding.

With the tools secured, Maria asked, "So we're going to the

kitchen next?"

"That is where Louisa wanted us to wait," Carrie agreed calmly.

Maria gave her a hard look, then giggled. "I should have known you'd formulate your own plans. What are we doing?"

Carrie grinned. "Have you ever helped the kitchen staff?"

"The soup smells good," Maria whispered. Her stomach gurgled in agreement.

"It's also heavy," Carrie said, hefting a tureen of the creamy bisque.

It had been simple to get assigned to the kitchen staff. Since Mrs. Wilkins, the cook, had expected them to be in the kitchen, it had not taken much to convince her that she had misheard her instructions—the two girls were not to wait in the kitchen, but help the kitchen maids wait on the tables.

Appropriate clothing had been given to the girls, with hissed warnings to not spill food on the freshly starched aprons. They had helped each other change and dress their hair. Carrie's temples throbbed from the tightness of her bun. She hoped it stayed put. Her hair was forever escaping any attempts to confine it.

Maria's hair had also been scraped into a bun, but what bothered her seemed to be the collar of her dress, which she kept tugging. Carrie had to admit that the maid's dress was uncomfortable and hot.

Once dressed, they had met Thornton, the butler. He'd given brusque instructions in their responsibilities that evening. Carrie and Maria found themselves with two other young women. Each had been assigned three people to serve at the table. There were also two footmen, to carry the heavy serving dishes. Thornton would be pouring wine for the guests and keeping a close eye on the lower servants.

"Here now, miss, that's my job," one of the footmen said, catching her picking up the tureen. He gently took it from her grasp and, when the butler opened the door, carried it into the dining room. The other footman followed with a second tureen. Both ladled soup into bowls, which the maids, Carrie and Maria included, conveyed to the table.

Carrie longed to check on her listening devices. Were they working? Had any fallen from their perches? She set her bowl in front of a guest and risked a peek at their face.

She gasped. "Lieutenant Beauchamp?"

The man stiffened and glanced at her. Then his eyes widened, and he whispered, lips barely moving, "Miss Wheelwright? What on Earth . . . ?"

Maria walked by and pinched Carrie's arm. Carrie looked away from Beauchamp and found Thornton, the butler, glaring at her.

"I beg your pardon, sir," she said quietly, and scurried back to the sideboard to collect another bowl of soup to deliver.

As she served the next guest, Carrie swept her eyes around the table, taking a full look at the guests. Lieutenant Beauchamp, whom she had met last year during the Russian agent debacle, was not wearing his naval uniform—decidedly unusual for a formal dinner. That was interesting. Her sister Louisa sat at the foot of the table, and Carrie assumed that the man at the head of the table was her husband, Joseph. Carrie had never met him, given the scandalous nature of their marriage and her parents' indecision of how to handle it. She didn't recognize anyone else, although she suspected that the man and woman who wore colour-coordinated outfits were minor royalty of some sort, given the deference they were being treated with.

Everyone served, the maids lined up silently along the wall, waiting for Thornton's signal to clear the dishes. Maria tugged at Carrie's sleeve and angled her chin at one of the guests. Carrie narrowed her eyes. Recognition came slowly. The Port of Vancouver harbour master.

Carrie dipped her head a fraction of an inch. Maria returned the minuscule nod. They were on the same page, then. Louisa hadn't disclosed the nature of the plot she was trying to gather evidence about, but with Lieutenant Beauchamp, out of uniform, and the harbour master present at dinner, Louisa's mysterious security matter had to concern the port.

The port was starting to flourish, finally, with the arrival of the railroad in Vancouver. With the coasts of Canada connected, Vancouver could serve as an alternate sea route to Asia from England. And if the work of the port was disrupted, maybe some of the steamships would divert to Seattle instead.

The logic was tenuous, and based on too few data points, but Carrie had learned last year that foreign powers were very interested in Vancouver's ports and shipping capabilities. Louisa suspected someone in this room of plotting to sabotage the port, and Carrie believed her.

While clearing and serving the next few courses, Carrie gleaned the names of her assigned guests. Lieutenant Beauchamp was going by the name of Mr. Dreighton. Women were seated on either side of him; one was an actress by the name of Miranda Royale, and the other was a middle-aged woman called Mrs. Drale.

In hurried, whispered exchanges, Maria shared the names of her guests: Louisa's husband, Joseph, who slurped his soup; Miss Pevensie, daughter of an American businessman; and Mr. Allenton, the assistant to the mayor of Vancouver.

Those were only half the guests, and Carrie despaired of uncovering the culprit or discovering any clues for her sister. The other two maids wouldn't talk to her, and Thornton constantly glared. At least she hadn't spilled food on her dress, unlike Maria, who had a small blot of dill sauce on her sleeve cuff. All in all, the only noteworthy item she had to report was that Louisa's husband slurped his soup.

As she reached over to deposit the dessert in front of Lieutenant Beauchamp, Mrs. Drale suddenly pushed her chair back and stood away from the table, jostling the small bowl from Carrie's hand. Thankfully, none of the pudding spilled on the snowy white tablecloth, but Beauchamp's spoon was knocked askew and slid over the edge.

Sighing, Carrie crouched to find the utensil. She picked it up and then noticed one of her listening devices perched above her head. She stared at it for a few seconds, then pulled it free from the table and stuffed it into her apron pocket. With Beauchamp sitting at this particular place, she reasoned, they didn't really need a device here; he could remember his conversations just as well. Besides, it was an interesting construct, and she wanted to poke at it at her own laboratory when she returned home. She was certain she could improve on the hasty design.

Humming, she stood up and quietly informed Beauchamp

that she would fetch him another spoon. Mrs. Drale, she saw, had a brief discussion with a footman, and then left the room entirely.

When Carrie returned with a new spoon for Beauchamp, Mrs. Drale had returned, but Joseph had left the room. Carrie hesitated, staring at the empty spot, then, feeling the burn of Thornton's disapproving glare, swiftly strode to Lieutenant Beauchamp and placed the spoon beside his pudding bowl.

Carrie sneaked a glance at Louisa. Her sister was speaking absently with her neighbour, the male minor royal, but her eyes were focused on Joseph's empty chair. She looked rather pale.

After the dessert course, the women, led by Louisa, stood from their chairs and glided from the dining room. They would have tea in the drawing room, while the men smoked cigars and drank alcohol stronger than wine in the dining room. Carrie watched the women leave, her stomach churning. Louisa had specifically requested that just the men be spied upon. Was that because she needed a device to listen to the men, while Louisa herself interrogated the women? Or because she had reason to suspect a man in particular? Carrie's gaze drifted to Joseph, who had returned during the dessert course and now passed around a box of cigars.

Still, her gut told her that the women deserved observation, too. "I need to be in the drawing room," she whispered to Maria.

Maria shook her head. "Thornton won't allow it. He doesn't like you, and Gertie is head maid."

"Louisa was wrong to focus solely on the men," Carrie said. "She needs me in there, even if she doesn't know it."

Maria grinned. "I have an idea."

She darted into the kitchen. Within moments, Carrie heard a resounding crash, a scream, and then lots of yelling. The men didn't even twitch, but Thornton looked up from pouring a whiskey for Mr. Allenton.

The kitchen door flew open, revealing Mrs. Wilkins, face flushed brick red and her eyes narrowed to murderous slits. Smears of bisque soup splotched her apron, dress, and face. "You'll need to take tea to the ladies," she said to Carrie, and stomped back to the kitchen.

Carrie followed, carefully stepping around the tiny scullery maid sweeping up broken crockery and avoiding eye contact with

Maria, who was sitting on the floor in a puddle of soup. Gertie sat next to her, crying into her apron, or perhaps wiping her face, which seemed to be covered entirely in creamy crab bisque.

In a few minutes, Carrie left the kitchen through a separate door and made her way to the drawing room. While she didn't dawdle, she didn't race toward her destination either. How could she get anyone to reveal incriminating information? Nobody talked to maids. She would only have a few minutes to uncover clues; once tea was served, she would be dismissed.

Louisa's relieved welcoming smile twisted sourly when Carrie entered the drawing room.

"What are you doing here?" she ground out through a stiff smile.

"Helping you. I'm not convinced the culprit is a man," Carrie murmured, placing the tray down on the table and helping Louisa set out cups.

Louisa's eyes widened, and her gaze flitted around the room, no doubt evaluating the women in a different light. She had been convinced that a man was behind the plot.

"What do you propose?" Louisa asked, pouring out tea.

"I've an idea. Follow my lead."

Once tea had been distributed and small cakes served, Carrie walked to the door. Halting, she turned around and said, "Oh, ma'am, just one more thing. I found this in the dining room. Perhaps it belongs to one of your guests?"

"You should have brought it to Thornton's attention, but very well. Bring it here." Louisa held out a hand.

From her apron pocket, Carrie pulled out the listening device and gave it to her sister.

"Why, it looks like a miniature player piano cylinder," Louisa exclaimed. She turned the tiny crank, and the room was filled with tinny, yet unmistakable, sounds of their dinner conversation. Carrie recognized Louisa's voice, the minor royal's voice, and Mrs. Drale's voice.

"What is that?" Mrs. Drale asked. "Where did it come from?"

"It fell from the table," Carrie said. "Maybe from someone's pocket?"

"But surely," said the minor royal's wife, "that is our conversation?" She stared at the listening device. "That is some kind of spying machine!"

An excited murmur rippled through the women.

"Spying machine?" Mrs. Drale repeated in a hard voice. "Mrs. Dalton, is the embassy in the habit of spying on its guests?"

"I don't have anything to do with this," Louisa said.

"What if they're all over the embassy?" Carrie asked loudly. "Listening to everything we say?"

In the sudden silence that blanketed the room, Mrs. Drale's horrified gasp sounded like cannon fire.

"Oh, dear," Carrie said, turning to Mrs. Drale, "weren't you called away from the table? You . . ." Carrie paused, thinking furiously. Why would she have left the dining room? The necessary? But why talk to the footman, then? The logical answer occurred to her, and Carrie smiled. "You received a telegram, didn't you?"

"Did you talk to the messenger in the hallway?" Louisa cautiously asked. "Or . . ."

"Read the telegram out loud!" both Carrie and Louisa shouted.

Mrs. Drale jumped to her feet and ran for the door, her cup of tea falling to the floor. Carrie charged after her. She grabbed Mrs. Drale's arm and yanked, but Mrs. Drale swung her other arm around and slapped Carrie in the face.

Carrie ignored the sting. Keeping hold of Mrs. Drale's arm, she butted her head against Mrs. Drale's shoulder and pushed. Unbalanced, Mrs. Drale toppled to the floor, Carrie sprawling down on top of her.

"What on Earth is happening here?"

Carrie looked up into the astonished face of Lieutenant Beauchamp.

Maria and Carrie had both changed into their own clothes, Maria smelling faintly of soup. The guests had been sent home, except Mrs. Drale, who had special rooms in the embassy.

"She tried to hold out on a confession," Beauchamp was saying, "but because you'd deduced she'd received a telegram, we were able to discover the remains. She'd tried to burn it, but enough scraps were legible for us to piece together the content. With that knowledge"—Beauchamp shrugged—"well, she saw the advantage of coming clean. We have men out hunting down her co-conspirators. The port's safe."

"What I don't understand," said Joseph slowly, "is that if you suspected a traitor among us, Louisa, why didn't you say something? We could have coordinated our efforts."

Louisa smiled weakly. "Oh, I . . . I . . ."

"She wanted to impress you, Joseph," Carrie said. "We Wheelwrights like to show off how clever we are."

Beauchamp let out a laugh, which he quickly turned into a cough.

"That's it exactly, darling," Louisa said. "We're dreadful show-offs. I suppose I just wanted to make you proud of me." She lowered her eyelashes and smiled bashfully.

Joseph flushed. "Oh! Well . . . of course, I'm proud of you. It was a job well done." He flashed an amused glance at Maria. "Although Miss Acevado and your sister may not be allowed back, if Mrs. Wilkins has anything to say about it."

Maria yawned.

Joseph slapped his thighs and stood up. "And it's getting late."

Beauchamp also stood. "I can escort the two young ladies home."

"Thank you, Lieutenant, that would be much appreciated," Louisa said, also rising.

They all migrated to the hallway, where Carrie, Maria, and Beauchamp were helped into coats.

"Carrie," Louisa murmured, gathering her in for a hug, "thank you. For everything."

"You owe me a favour, Louisa," Carrie whispered into her ear. Louisa stiffened and started to pull away, so Carrie hastily added, "You and Joseph should come to dinner on Sunday."

"I'd—I'd like that, Carrie," Louisa said.

They embraced for several more seconds. When they parted, Beauchamp grasped Carrie's elbow and led her out the door, past the guards, Maria on his other arm.

"Carrie, what was that bunk about Louisa showing off for her husband?" Maria demanded.

Carrie shot a glance at the guards. "I was trying to save my sister's marriage, because she seems fond of him."

"Ah," Beauchamp said. "I begin to understand."

"You see, Maria," Carrie said quietly, "she was afraid Joseph was behind the plot, and if I helped her, rather than, say, Lieutenant Beauchamp, then she might be able to foil the scheme without getting Joseph in trouble."

"Oh," Maria said. "Why didn't she just say so? I could have told her that someone who slurps their soup like he does can't sneak around blowing up ports."

After a stunned moment, Beauchamp and Carrie burst out laughing.

DISCORD ON HARMONIA

Originally published in *Brave New Girls: Tales of Heroines Who Hack*. Brave New Girls, 2018.

My kid wanted a story about a girl living on Mars, and this is the result—my second story published in the Brave New Girls anthology series.

DISCORD ON HARMONIA

The magnetic tape crackled and snapped shut, pinching Pippa Mwangi's finger. "Dust and rocks!" she yelped, prying the strip open. She tossed it aside and sat back in her chair, glaring at it. The neodymium metal made strong permanent magnets, but the tape was proving to be difficult to work with. Maybe her hope to use it for exo-suit fasteners was misguided. She sighed. Maybe she was wasting her time.

Her work table was littered with magnets and tools. The best thing about both of her moms working for a mining corporation was that Pippa always had samples of neodymium on hand. Harmonia Mining Corp was supportive of their employees' families—they had to be, with Earthers being reluctant to move to Mars. The mining corp provided free housing in the domed city of Harmonia for their employees, and they offered generous scholarships for their employees' children.

Pippa frowned at her magnetic tape. "Maybe heat . . . ?" she murmured, leaning forward and reaching past her electromagnet for her mini-fuser.

The room shook, and the tools on her table rattled. Pippa glanced up at the ceiling. "Jeeves?"

"Harmonia Dome is under attack," replied the house's artificial intelligence system.

The room shook again, and a warning klaxon blared.

"Dome breach," Jeeves intoned. "Please observe breach protocol."

Pippa froze for a second. While she had drilled for Dome breaches, she didn't remember the Dome ever having one. Jeeves repeated his warning, and she squeaked, grabbing her magnetic tape, toolkit, and the tools scattered on the table surface. She wasn't going to the emergency shelter without something to keep her busy. She'd go nuts.

"Please observe breach protocol," the AI instructed for a third time.

"I got it, Jeeves. Chill."

Stuffing her tools into her toolkit, Pippa dashed to the main entryway, where the exo-suits were stored. They were meticulously clean and neat—for just this kind of emergency, when her life might depend on her exo-suit. As she stuffed her feet into her boots and tugged her suit on, she asked, "Jeeves, what is the status of my moms? Is the mine okay?"

As Jeeves accessed the system, Pippa checked the seals around her boots.

"Harmonia Mine is also under attack," Jeeves said. "No data available on casualties."

Pippa closed her eyes. If the mine was also under fire, then the perpetrators of this attack had to be Adrestia Mining Corp. The Adrestia mine had been shut down a few months ago due to a cataclysmic tunnel failure. Since then, they'd been trying to negotiate mining rights with Harmonia Mining Corporation. Apparently, they were now employing a more forceful strategy.

Opening her eyes, Pippa frowned. She couldn't imagine how desperate the people of Adrestia must feel to launch an attack against another Dome. It wasn't a smart move, especially against Harmonia, a larger and more prosperous mining corp. Still, she thought, as another weapon shook the Dome, scared people could do horrible things.

Pippa shook her head. She had to focus. There wasn't much she could do about Adrestia trying to take over Harmonia Dome and its mine. She wasn't a pilot, or a member of HarSec, or a researcher. She didn't even have the equipment to go to the mine and help her mothers and the other miners. All she could really do was stay safe, as her moms would want. Just like she'd trust that her moms were following their own safety protocols.

She quickly snapped on the rest of the exo-suit. Then she pulled a wide headband over her head, forcing her cloud of copper-coloured curls out of her face. As she put on her helmet, she caught a glimpse of herself in the visor and frowned, not liking the frightened-bunny stare of her brown eyes. The suit's computer system switched on, obliterating her reflection.

Across the screen scrolled the words: *For full suit access, please identify yourself.*

"Phillipa Mwangi," she said.

Full access granted.

Pippa sealed the helmet into place, relaxing as the computer screen displayed the proper flow of oxygen into her suit. Breach protocol strongly suggested using canned oxygen in case of sudden exposure to Mars's atmosphere. Then, she wrapped her toolkit around her waist, securing it to the exo-suit's belt. Finally, she pulled on the suit's gloves, snapping the seals shut.

"Enable external speakers," she said to the suit's computer, then continued, "Jeeves? Where do I report?" Her voice sounded tinny and small, emerging from her suit.

"Recommend you—"

An explosion rocked the apartment, and Jeeves's voice fizzed and popped before fading out entirely. Pippa stumbled and fell.

Housing breach, flashed across her visor's computing screen as metal screeched and clunked. One of the emergency barriers had slammed into place, sealing off a portion of the apartment.

"Where?" she asked.

A map appeared on the screen. A flashing red dot pinpointed the breach.

Pippa huffed. "Figures it would be my room."

Shoving aside images of what the harsh Martian landscape would do to her things, Pippa stood up. "Computer, locate nearest shelter."

The map of her apartment winked out, to be replaced by a map of her Dome level. A green dot blinked, indicating the nearest emergency shelter.

"Thank you." She cleared her throat. "Jeeves, lower the emergency habitat shield once I've left."

She'd barely taken a step outside the entrance when another

massive metal door *thunk*ed into place, protecting the rest of the habitat level from the breach in her apartment.

How many other metal doors had been lowered? How many sections of the Dome had been breached?

Her chest felt tight. If the Dome was taking this much damage, how was the mine faring?

Amber emergency-lighting strips along the floor illuminated the way to the shelter. The corridor was eerily empty. Pippa's breath hitched. Was she the last to seek shelter? Or was she sealed off from other people? She quickened her pace but refrained from breaking into a run. She'd use up her oxygen supply faster if she ran. Still, she didn't want to dawdle—she didn't want the shelter to fill up before she arrived.

She hugged the wall as it curved, and crashed into another person, getting knocked to the floor for the second time in the span of minutes.

Pippa scanned her visor display for problems with her suit's integrity. The numbers all registered green. "Good suit," she whispered, clambering to her feet.

The other person had also been knocked down. Pippa extended a hand, which the other accepted.

"Sorry about that," Pippa said as she helped the person to their feet. "Do you need help finding the shelter? I think you're going the wrong way."

"I'm not going the wrong way," retorted the stranger. "I'm reporting for duty. We're under attack." She tapped her chest, and Pippa dutifully examined the Harmonia Security patch.

"You're a pilot?" she asked, scanning the uniform. It was the familiar cobalt blue and crimson-trimmed suit, but it was a very poor fit, bagging at the knees, across her torso, and at the elbows. Rust-red Martian dust smeared the legs and splotched the helmet.

Pippa leaned forward and peered into the helmet. A pale girl with green-brown eyes stared back at her. Damp strands of mouse-brown hair clung to her forehead and cheeks. Pippa shook her head. "You're not in Security. You're my age!"

The girl grimaced. "Okay, so I'm not a pilot. I still need to get to the hangar."

The corridor shook as another weapon found its mark on the

Dome. Pippa's readouts still registered green, indicating that this section was still secure. "Look," she said, "the hangar isn't going to be safe. Let's go—" She reached for the girl's arm.

"No!" The girl jerked away. "You don't understand. I have to get down there. My little brother—I was supposed to watch him, and he's not here." She pulled at her blue exo-suit. "Our mom's in HarSec. He likes to hang around the ships."

Pippa pursed her lips. "I didn't think kids were allowed in HarSec's hangar."

The girl's eyebrows scrunched together. "It's my responsibility," she muttered.

Pippa shrugged. "All right. Well . . . Good luck." She wheeled past the girl, moving toward the shelter. It didn't seem right to let that girl wander around alone while the Dome was under attack. Maybe she should have dragged her to the shelter—rescued her against her will.

Pippa frowned. Something nagged at her thoughts. *Dragged . . .*

A resounding *thunk-thunk* echoed in the corridor. Then a scream.

"Dust and rocks," Pippa cursed, pausing. When whimpers reached her ears, she turned and walked swiftly to the sounds.

Metal barriers had descended, cutting the corridor off from another section. Pippa gulped. A major breach.

The girl was curled up on the floor next to the barriers.

"Are you all right?" Pippa called, breaking into a trot.

The girl looked up. "I'm stuck."

"Better than crushed," Pippa said. The girl smiled weakly.

Pippa crouched next to her. "What happened?" The excess material on the suit's leg was pinned beneath the metal barrier. Pippa tugged at it gently, but it was firmly caught. "Were you trying to beat the barriers? It's a good thing the suit is too big for you. You could have been killed."

The girl grunted and crossed her arms.

"Dust." Pippa fumbled with her toolkit. "I'm going to have to tear your suit."

Gasping, the girl stared at Pippa. "What?"

"I have a repair patch. Don't panic." Pippa selected a small knife from her kit. "I'm Pippa, by the way." She punctured the suit and slit the material.

"I'm Mindy."

The corridor rocked again. Pippa's computer display flashed yellow, and the primary lighting flickered and dimmed. The walls in this area were weakening. She needed to fix Mindy's suit immediately, before they had bigger problems to worry about.

"Hurry up!" Mindy cried.

Pippa finished cutting the suit, leaving a dusty fragment of fabric stuck under the barrier. She put the knife away, fingers brushing her standard suit repair patch. She hesitated, flicking a glance at Mindy's dusty suit, and passed over it, taking out instead the roll of neodymium magnetic tape and her mini-fuser.

"I've never seen patch fabric like that," Mindy said.

"It's . . . new," Pippa said. Pinching the edges of the suit together, Pippa applied the magnetic tape to form a new seam. As it had done on her table, the edges started to curl. "Hold that," she ordered Mindy, not wanting to suffer another pinched finger on top of everything else.

When Mindy had a firm grip on the makeshift seam, Pippa switched on her mini-fuser. She guided the mini-fuser over the tape, hoping it would force the adhesive to attach to Mindy's suit. As the tape bonded to the suit, a smile spread over her face. She hadn't been wasting her time experimenting with the magnetic tape.

"It looks okay," Mindy said, running her fingers along the new seam. "Thank you."

Pippa cocked her head. "My computer says it's tight." She stood up.

Mindy also scrambled to her feet, wincing. She leaned against the barrier, not putting any weight on the leg that had nearly been smashed. "Pippa, would you come with me? I obviously need help." She waved a hand at her patched suit.

I should drag her to the shelter. But if I'm right, the hangar is the best place to be. Pippa sighed. "Sure, Mindy, I'll go with you."

The dot representing the shelter still blinked insistently on her computer display. "Stairs," Pippa said.

The display shifted, showing her the staircase.

"Right, let's go, Mindy," Pippa said. "Hopefully the stairs aren't blocked."

Mindy snorted. "With the way my luck's been, don't get your hopes up."

The transport level—which included HarSec's hangar, the mining corporation's hangar, personal docking bays, and the inter-dome transit system station—was located on the lowest level of Harmonia Dome. That meant four flights of stairs. At least they were moving down and not climbing up, and the breach klaxon was muted.

Even with the relative ease of descent, Mindy's injured leg slowed them. It took a lot longer to reach the transport level than Pippa had planned.

Here were the signs of bustling confusion she'd expected on the habitat level. People rushing to various bays, some in exo-suits, some not; the rumble of numerous vehicles; the strobing warning lights and annoying klaxon. A brilliant scarlet X illuminated the doors leading to the inter-dome transport.

Pippa groaned. The train was a logical target if their attackers were trying to prevent escape. The next likely target would be the security hangars, to forestall defence. Of course, some of the pilots would have been on patrol; they wouldn't all have been grounded and possibly trapped by the attack.

Tearing her eyes from the inter-dome transport bay and the ominous red X, Pippa tugged on Mindy's sleeve. "Let's go, while we can get there. Harmonia Security hangar," Pippa said, and her computer immediately produced a new map, with the green dot now indicating the requested location.

If the main transport corridor had been busy, it was nothing compared to HarSec's hangar. Dozens of the blocky, emerald security ships, designed for the minimal atmosphere of Mars, were getting prepped for flight, with mechanics and pilots crawling all over them. Mechanic carts buzzed around from ship to ship, offering assistance to their human counterparts. Nobody spared a glance for Pippa and Mindy.

Mindy grabbed Pippa's arm as she stood on tiptoe, craning her head. "I see him! There's the little stinker." She pointed to an area near the main hangar doors.

Pippa stared at the cluster of pilots, mechanics, and staff. She didn't see a kid—but she hadn't expected to, not really. But she did see a lot of vulnerable adults shepherding ships out of the hangar. The bay door spiralled open, and two ships fired thrusters and flew through the opening. The door cycled shut. Although she couldn't see it, Pippa knew a second door would now open for the ships, sending them outside the Dome. Two more of the vibrant green ships queued up for their final safety checks.

"I don't see him," Pippa said, playing along with Mindy's lie. She reached into her tool kit and groped for her electromagnet. Finding it, she slipped it out and held it alongside her thigh, out of Mindy's sightline.

"I do," Mindy said. She patted Pippa's arm. "Thanks for your help." She limped forward, reaching for her rucksack.

"Nope, I don't think so," Pippa whispered, pressing the power button on her electromagnet and directing the head at Mindy's leg.

Mindy halted, her injured leg stuck in place.

The electromagnet jerked in Pippa's hand, and she lurched forward a step. "Dust," she muttered.

Her face twisted in confusion, Mindy yanked at the metal seam on her pants. "What did you do?" she yelled.

It would be impossible to resist the pull between the electromagnet and the neodymium tape on Mindy's suit. Instead, Pippa rushed Mindy. The girls collided, Mindy's leg sweeping up to meet the electromagnet in Pippa's hand. Then they toppled, Mindy landing awkwardly on Pippa.

Pippa grinned up into Mindy's scowling face. "Isn't my neodymium magnetic tape the best? It'll make great exo-suit fasteners."

"You've ruined everything," Mindy spat. She pulled something out of her rucksack. "Victory for Adrestia!" she screamed.

"Bomb!" Pippa yelled.

She grappled for the object in Mindy's hand. Mindy kneed her in the guts and, when Pippa curled her knees up, drove an elbow into Pippa's visor. Kicking her legs out, Pippa rolled, forcing Mindy onto her back. Then Pippa grabbed Mindy's wrist and squeezed, slamming the hand into the concrete floor, ignoring the pain that sizzled across her knuckles.

Strong hands grasped her shoulders, and she panicked, flailing, until words penetrated her helmet.

"We got it, we got it. You can let go."

Panting, Pippa dropped Mindy's hand and allowed herself to be lifted off the girl, but the magnets wouldn't allow for complete separation. Mindy's leg dangled from Pippa's hand like a bizarre extra limb.

Breath shuddering out on a weak chuckle, Pippa pressed the power button on the electromagnet. Mindy groaned when her foot smacked the floor, jolting the injured leg. Pippa returned the electromagnet to its sheath in her toolkit.

"What's this about?"

Pippa was relieved to see the new arrival: a captain, by the number of pips on her collar. She wasn't wearing an exo-suit, and her cobalt uniform was pristine and the creases sharp. Wisps of black hair peeked out from under her cap. Her mouth pressed into a thin line as her dark eyes darted from Pippa to Mindy.

Pippa couldn't help smiling. "Hi, Captain. I'm Pippa Mwangi from Habitat Level Four. I found this girl and guided her down here. She fed me a story about searching for her kid brother, but her story didn't make sense, so I kept her under observation until I could confirm my suspicions. As she threatened us with the bomb, she yelled something about Adrestia. I think she was sent to sabotage Harmonia Security while the Adrestia ships pummelled our Dome."

An ensign raced up to them. "Captain Zhao!"

The captain turned aside, and she and the ensign held a muted conversation.

"You knew?" Mindy asked. "You planned that magnet thing?"

"Of course, I knew. Your uniform is dirty," Pippa said. "You've obviously been *outside*. And the dust on the legs suggested you'd been dragged. Or rather, that someone wearing that exo-suit had been dragged around outside, since the suit wasn't tailored for you and you didn't seem to have access to the suit's computer. So, where had you come from, if you'd been outside with someone else's exo-suit?" She grimaced. "From one of the breaches in the Dome, after you'd killed a Security pilot. Which made you part of the hostile force."

The people holding Mindy grumbled and laughed. The laughter had a rough edge.

Captain Zhao rejoined them. "Please escort our saboteur to

the holding cells on Level Two." As Mindy was led away, the captain waved off the personnel hovering around Pippa. "I'll show Miss Mwangi out."

She gently cupped Pippa's elbow and steered her to the exit. "Thank you, Miss Mwangi, for your efforts today. She was indeed carrying a bomb." They halted by the doors. "I'd like to talk more about what you did, but the hangar isn't safe right now and I'm busy with defences."

"Wait!" Pippa blurted. "Can you tell me what's happening at the mine?"

Captain Zhao half-smiled. "The mine was attacked, but the mining transports and our patrol ships fought them off. No casualties have been suffered."

Pippa grinned, a weight lifting off her shoulders. Her moms were all right. "Thanks, Captain."

"Thank *you*, Pippa," Captain Zhao said. "Now, please find an emergency shelter to wait out the last of the skirmish. Now that our ships are mobilized, it shouldn't be too long."

As the captain strode back toward the ships, barking orders, Pippa left the hangar bay. Far fewer people were scurrying through the main corridor, and she navigated the crowds easily, following the emergency lighting strips to the nearest shelter.

Her stomach ached a little from where Mindy had kicked her, but she smiled as she settled in for the wait. She would have to ask Captain Zhao for the return of the magnetic tape. She'd been wrong, after all. She *had* contributed to the protection of Harmonia Dome.

SHOULDERING THE BURDEN

Originally published in *Mrs. Claus: Not the Fairy Tale They Say*, edited by Rhonda Parrish. World Weaver Press, 2017.

Steampunk, but make it Christmas. Or at least New Year's. "Shouldering the Burden" combines many things I love, with a nod to my Greek ancestry and heritage. At the time of this writing, the British Museum has new trustees who are adamantly opposed to returning the Parthenon marbles to Greece.

SHOULDERING THE BURDEN

Phaedra stood on the deck of the *Northern Queen*. The salt-heavy air tickled her nose, and she sighed with contentment. It had been a long time since she'd been to Greece, her homeland. She'd accepted the special gift-bearer assignment as an excuse for a visit—and to banish her nightmares.

The dock workers called to them, and Phaedra answered. Then she translated the Greek instructions into Dutch for the elves, who quickly complied with the docking directions.

Since it was night, the elves hadn't bothered with glamours to hide pointed ear-tips or to add inches to their height. As the airship bumped gently into its docking berth, the elves slithered over the side and clambered down the ropes, securing the *Northern Queen* to the spindly dock that extended from the Piraeus Airship Tower.

Despite the commotion, the sobbing persisted. Incessant, heavy sobbing. Phaedra heard it every night, awake or asleep. It haunted her during the day, a ringing in her ears that never faded.

Catching sight of the customs agent, Phaedra summoned a welcoming smile. The official came aboard, navigating the gangplank with ease, and Phaedra felt a twinge of guilt for the lies she'd have to tell him—he seemed pleasant, if tired.

"*Kalí chroniá!*" she said warmly. It was New Year's Eve, and a wish for a good year was more appropriate than Merry Christmas, even if she was on a gift-bearing mission.

He blinked. "But you speak Greek so well! Surely, you are a daughter of our fair country."

His voice lilted, not quite a question, and Phaedra didn't wonder at his doubt. Even in the night, the elves' fair complexions and hair were striking. They darted around the deck of the airship like will o' the wisps. She smiled and beckoned the customs agent closer to one of the gas lamps.

"My husband and I live in the North now, so our airship is crewed with sailors from that land, but I am Greek, yes. How kind of you to not remark on my rusty words!" Phaedra laughed and touched his arm.

He relaxed. In the light, her bronze skin and dark eyes were arresting. Her wavy black hair, shot with strands of iron-grey and pinned up in a complicated knot, and her dress, high quality wool, spoke of a genteel woman of means.

"How wonderful to have you back home, then," he said with a smile. "You understand I need to see your manifest and travel log?"

"Of course," Phaedra said, "I have them here." She handed him the ledger.

"Oh . . ." The customs agent frowned. "You were in England?"

Phaedra kept her smile firmly in place. "Yes, shopping. I couldn't come home without gifts!"

"Of course, of course, but there was a theft from the museum there." He gave her an apologetic shrug. "We are supposed to search all ships coming from England. They've put out an alert all over the continent."

"Of course," Phaedra said. "What a shame you must stay late tonight, when your family must be waiting for the New Year to come. The *Northern Queen* is quite large."

He shifted his weight, tapping the ledger with nervous fingers. "Er . . . yes." He stared at her, the Greek woman with a stout, matronly figure and a warm smile, and cleared his throat. "Well, I'm sure everything is in order here. Why waste our time searching the ship of a daughter of Greece?" He signed her travel record and handed the ledger back to her.

As he disembarked, he turned, waved, and wished her a Happy New Year.

"Any sign of pursuit from England?"

Phaedra gasped and clutched her chest. Heart pounding, she swivelled. "Annika, you startled me!"

Annika bowed. "I'm sorry, Mrs. Claus, I thought you heard me approach." The elf folded her arms. "This gift-delivery would be easier if we used the sleigh. Its magic is stronger than the airship's."

Phaedra sighed. "This is Ágios Vassílis' night, and we're here with his permission. He's allowed us an airship, but no sleigh and no reindeer. That's not how it's done in Greece."

She and Nicholas had offered to give the statue to Vassílis for him to deliver, but he'd declined. He believed Phaedra, the only one who could hear the crying, should have the honour of delivery.

"We're taking the runabout to the Acropolis, Annika. It's so tiny that it's less likely to be noticed and it'll feel more . . . sleigh-like."

The elf snorted. "It will be slow and clumsy."

At that moment, half a dozen elves came up from belowdecks, carrying an oil-cloth swathed object. The marble statue was heavy, and the elves grunted and muttered. Phaedra did not speak Elvish but, judging by the scandalized look on Annika's face, suspected a few not-so-jolly words were dropping from their tongues.

"To answer your earlier question, there's no sign of any pursuit. They've discovered the theft, though. The customs agent had instructions to search for it."

Annika nodded. "We'll leave once it's loaded then?" She patted the leather satchel slung over her shoulder. "I am ready, are you?"

Phaedra smiled, indicating her dress—dark green with holly leaves and berries embroidered around the cuffs and hem—with a flourish. While most of her responsibilities at the North Pole involved managing the compound, the image of the gift-bearer was important. Useful tools, not important to the image, but good to have around, were discreetly tucked away—a collapsed telescoping parasol in one boot and a multi-tool in a pocket.

"Hmm," Annika said. "You're missing something." She reached into her satchel and pulled out a red velvet cloak trimmed with white rabbit fur.

"It's warm enough, I didn't think I'd need it, but you're right." Phaedra wrapped the cloak around her shoulders and fastened the clasp. "Should we bring Muninn, do you think?"

Annika grinned. "Already thought of that, Phaedra. He's in the runabout waiting for us."

The elves had finished lashing the statue to the runabout and called to Phaedra and Annika. They hastened to the side of the airship, where the runabout was snugged up tight to the *Northern Queen*. The statue, still wrapped in cloth, sat in the prow. Jan sat in the stern, hands on the controls for the rudder, fins, and air balloon. A massive clockwork raven perched on a bench. It stretched its wings and cawed at them in greeting.

"I am pleased to assist with the gift-bearing mission!" he croaked.

Phaedra smiled. She was fond of the mechanical bird. He helped watch the reindeer herds during the winter, since they grazed far south of the Pole, but Phaedra had felt he might come in handy during their mission, so he'd been temporarily pulled from that duty.

Phaedra and Annika climbed into the runabout and settled onto their bench. The nearly-silent purr of the engine indicated that the magical engine was at work, not the steam-powered one. Phaedra smiled in approval. They wouldn't be invisible, but they could move as quietly as Nick's sleigh.

"Let's take her out, Jan. Head for the Acropolis," Phaedra said.

Jan nodded. The ropes securing the runabout were released, and the runabout drifted from the *Northern Queen*. The purr of the engine grew into a *putt-putt-putt*, and the smaller airship turned and sailed north-east.

Their course was simple to plot since their destination dominated the skyline. Bathed in moonlight, the marble structures on the Acropolis gleamed ghostly-white.

Phaedra sighed another happy sigh. It felt remarkably pleasant to be in her homeland, speaking Greek with people other than Nick. She wondered if they might extend their visit a little longer and have some food. Fresh fish perhaps? The North Pole had begun to modernize, and they had built a wonderfully ornate glass conservatory with a steeply pitched roof, chock-full of edible plants. And while it was wonderful having fresh Kalamata olives, she was still stuck with salt fish and beef during the long winter.

Maybe . . . maybe she could just stay here awhile? Not return right away to the Pole? The notion was terrifying in its simplicity and attraction.

"Penny for your thoughts, Phaedra?" Annika asked.

"Oh!" Phaedra waved a hand. "I was thinking about staying here for a few extra days . . . or weeks."

"Stay?" Annika echoed. "Weeks? But there's so much work to be done!"

Phaedra's shoulders sagged. There was a lot, but it wasn't the work, it was the *responsibility*: she supervised harvesting, planting, and food preparation; coordinated household chores; scheduled elf work shifts and reindeer herd migrations; organized weaving and sewing; sorted Nick's mail; and oversaw construction projects—two this year, a new reindeer barn and a high-tech observatory, to better monitor Nick's flight on Christmas Eve. And those were just the tasks associated with support! She assisted with the toy manufacturing and reindeer training as well.

At the North Pole, a bundle of keys, one for each door of the complex, hung from a ring on Phaedra's sturdy belt. Each year, as the gift-bearer operation grew, more elves arrived to assist, more buildings were added, and more keys slid onto the ring on her belt. Her lower back ached most days from the great key-ring dangling from her waist.

What would they do without her?

"You're right, Annika," Phaedra said, managing a brief upturn of her mouth, more of a twitch than a smile. "We have to get started on next year's operation."

And yet, as she watched the Acropolis creep closer, she still wondered, what if—?

Jan slowed the tiny airship as they approached the Acropolis. "Which temple?" he called.

"That one!" Phaedra yelled, pointing. "The Erechtheion, the

one with the women!"

The sobbing that had plagued her for so long was much louder now, a keening that made her head ache.

Jan stabilized the runabout and threw ropes over the side. Phaedra grimaced. He wasn't expecting her to shimmy down one of those ropes, was he?

She sighed in relief when Jan climbed down the ropes himself, tying the airship to the temple. As he climbed back up, hand over hand, Phaedra pinned a small brooch to her cloak. The brooch had aethergraph capabilities, and she could use it to talk to Jan.

When Jan was back aboard the runabout, he unrolled a rope ladder. In Phaedra's opinion, the ladder wasn't much better than just sliding down a rope, but she made it to the ground without disaster. Annika dropped down beside her a few minutes later.

Next, Jan lowered the statue. Although it was attached by ropes, it was North Pole magic, which eased the delivery of all manner of gifts all over the world, that kept the airship steady and saw the massive statue safely lowered to the ground.

Together, Annika and Phaedra rolled the wrapped statue to the southern porch of the Erechtheion. Instead of stately, Ionic columns, like those on the northern porch, here five marble women supported the structure with a gaping hole where a sixth should stand. The Caryatids.

Phaedra patted the heavy bundle. "Almost there, lady. I can't believe they locked you up in a museum."

The sobbing abruptly broke off. Hushed words fill her head instead.

"Careful."

"Attend."

"Beware."

"Caution."

"Guard."

Phaedra stared at the five Caryatids. They hadn't moved, but she was certain the whispered warnings had come from them.

"Annika, did you hear that?"

Annika had not wasted time in starting to unwrap the statue. She stopped sawing at a rope with her small knife and looked up. "Rodents, don't you think?"

"Rodents . . . ?" Phaedra held her breath and cocked her head, straining to hear the least sound. Ah, there. A sort of scrabbling, scratching sound. Under ordinary circumstances, she'd be happy to assume mice or rats were the culprits, but she doubted the Caryatids would have warned her about mice.

"Who's there?" she called. She brought her hands together and concentrated. On a gift-bearing night, her North Pole magic was enhanced and she could cast small spells. A ball of light formed between her hands. Parting them, she blew a gentle stream of air at the light. The globe floated away from her, toward the shadows of the temple.

Something cackled. In the silvery light of Phaedra's globe, malformed, black shapes writhed and capered.

"By the Pole, what *are* those things?" Annika gasped.

The creatures shrank from the light, but Phaedra caught glimpses of goats' legs, horns, tusks, spindly tails, and red eyes. She gulped. "I think those are *kallikantzaroi*." At Annika's puzzled shrug, Phaedra added, "Goblins. They only come above ground during the twelve days of Christmas."

Annika resumed hacking at the ropes. "Let's do this quickly then, before they decide to pester us."

Phaedra knelt, pulling her own multi-tool from her pocket.

The Caryatids hissed in her mind, and Phaedra jerked her head up. An inky black thing, the size of a badger, leapt at her. Its mouth gaped open, displaying rows of jagged teeth.

Phaedra pulled her telescoping parasol out of her boot. She raised the metal rod and batted the goblin aside.

Another capering goblin bounded from the shadows.

"Keep at those ropes, Annika!" Phaedra shouted, struggling to her feet. She struck this *kallikantzaros* too as it jumped for her face. It shrieked, smacking into the temple wall and falling to the ground.

Phaedra pressed the brooch pinned to her velvet cloak, activating its aethergraph. "I need Muninn!"

"Yes, Mrs. Claus!" came the crackly response from Jan.

Two *kallikantzaroi* jumped her at once. As she conked one on the head with the parasol rod, the second climbed her shoulders and clawed her face.

She screamed, scrabbling at the goblin.

A raucous caw announced Muninn's arrival. His talons

clenched around the goblin and tore it free of Phaedra's shoulders. Muninn strove for altitude. Once he'd risen several feet in the air, he dropped the *kallikantzaros*. It hit the dusty ground with a wet thwap. Muninn cawed, circled, and dove again at the horde of *kallikantzaroi*.

Phaedra staggered, touching her injured cheek. It was wet, and she took away her hand and stared at the blood on her fingers. "What do they want?" she muttered, wiping the blood onto her skirt. The parasol rod slipped in the sweaty grip of her other hand.

"*Mischief,*" echoed in her head.

"*Devilment.*"

"*Discord.*"

"*Chaos.*"

"*Pain.*"

Still more of the goblins emerged from the dark. Phaedra risked a quick glance at Annika. The elf had finished cutting the ropes on one end—sandaled feet peeked out from the loosening oil cloth—and moved to the head, sawing at the ropes there.

A cluster of *kallikantzaroi* gambolled forward, gibbering, long tongues snaking from their mouths. Muninn swooped and dove at them, talons extended. He clutched two, while his mighty wings knocked over the rest.

With cries of "*Danger!*" filling her head, Phaedra tore her eyes away from the mechanical raven. A goblin crouched in front of her, jaw unhinged, fangs glistening. She depressed the button on her parasol rod. It extended another foot, and several smaller spokes popped out from the main rod. Fabric unfurled from the spokes, and within seconds, Phaedra held a beautiful, yet sturdy parasol. She used it as a shield, so that the canopy protected her face and body.

Venom splattered against her parasol. The fabric hissed as the acid burned holes in it.

Before the snake-like goblin could spit at her again, Phaedra pressed the button a second time, collapsing the parasol. She rushed the goblin and hit it on the head with the metal rod. After it keeled over, she stooped, picked it up by one cloven hoof, and hurled it at the Erechtheion.

"Got it!" Annika yelled.

Phaedra spun on her heel and dashed to Annika and the sixth Caryatid. Holding out her hand, she concentrated again. "Come on, need to finish the delivery," she murmured. A weak breeze swirled around her hand. She blew on it, and it flowed from her to the prone statue.

The Caryatid rose from the ground, her oil-cloth covering falling away as she floated to the porch and her five sisters.

Dimly, Phaedra could hear Muninn screeching and cursing as he struggled against the *kallikantzaroi*. But drowning out the sounds of the world around her was a chorus of feminine voices, the five Caryatids rejoicing in the return of their long-lost sister.

The sixth statue slid into her spot, the marble grinding as her head and feet settled into her space, and her voice joined the choir. The sisters' song reached a triumphant crescendo and cut off. As the resonance of the last note rang, a blinding flash of golden light burst from the six Caryatids. Phaedra threw her arms in front of her face, stumbled, and fell to the ground. Shrill screams of pain sounded behind her. Gradually, the light faded, and Phaedra lowered her arms.

The six Caryatids stood in place, dignified women. Important women, as they were holding up a roof with their heads. They weren't human, but they weren't quite stone, either.

"What a heavy load they bear," Phaedra whispered. Tears pricked her eyes.

She stood, wincing as her ankle twinged. Next to her, Annika rubbed her eyes and blinked.

"Is it done?" the elf asked. "Where are those fiends?"

"Gone, I think," Phaedra said. "I heard them screaming. That light probably hurt them."

Annika grunted. "She looks good."

"She does." Phaedra smiled. "Happy, even."

"I'm exhausted," Annika said, yawning. "I can hardly wait to see my bed. Let's go, Phaedra. We'll be back at the North Pole before dawn."

Phaedra hesitated. What harm to stay? To enjoy the sun? No snow, no ice, no lutefisk. It was tempting. She could practically feel the sun warming her face, could taste tangy goat cheese.

"Phaedra?"

Annika stood at the rope ladder, Muninn cradled in her arms.

One of the raven's wings hung crookedly, a few talons were missing, and acid burns mottled his body. But his eyes were bright and he cawed.

"I defeated the goblin menace," Muninn croaked.

Chuckling, Phaedra looked again at the Caryatids. The sixth had been pampered and adored in a museum, admired by countless people. Yet, Phaedra had felt her joy at rejoining her sisters, at taking up her share of the burden.

Phaedra squared her shoulders. "Coming, Annika! Do you need me to carry Muninn? He's nearly as big as you!"

As she climbed out of the runabout and onto the deck of the *Northern Queen*, Phaedra knew immediately that something had happened. The elves were bouncing, eyes twinkling and cheeks flushed.

Phaedra sniffed, but didn't detect the odor of spirits. "What's got into everyone?"

The elves all began speaking at once. Phaedra could only decipher snatches of sentences.

"—didn't see anything—"

"—suddenly—"

"—what humans feel—"

"Come look!"

That last was clear enough, and Phaedra allowed herself to be tugged to the captain's room. A large table dominated the cabin; it was the hub of the ship, where meals were shared, meetings held, and courses plotted.

It was covered in food. Platters of cheese and olives, baked fish, dolmathes, and souvlaki. Bowls of tzatziki and salads. Loaves of bread placed at regular intervals along the length of the table. In the centre, towering over the other dishes, was a tiered dessert stand, filled with baklava, kourabiedes, loukomi, and nuts. A feast.

Phaedra gawked. "How—?"

"We don't know," said an elf. "It just . . . appeared. We didn't see anyone, Mrs. Claus!"

"We weren't asleep!" chimed another.

"There's a letter," Annika said, stretching an arm to pluck an envelope that was propped against the tiered dessert plates. She handed it to Phaedra.

My Dear Phaedra,

Kalí chroniá – Happy New Year!

Ágios Vassílis

A gift for her—a taste of her homeland. Tears pricked her eyes again. "Thank you, Ágios Vassílis," she murmured, pressing the letter to her lips.

She slipped the letter into her pocket. "All right, everyone, let's eat!" She caught Annika's gaze and smiled. "No one will notice if we're a little late returning home."

Annika snorted, plucking a small square of loukami from the dessert plates.

Phaedra laughed. Gift-bearing—and the responsibilities that went with it—was good work, hard work, and she was proud to be part of it. But she and Nick needed to talk about periodic pleasure trips. Unlike the Caryatids, she wasn't made of stone.

FLYING THE COOP

Originally published in *Corvidae*, edited by Rhonda Parrish. World Weaver Press, 2015.

True story: I decided last minute to submit a story for the Corvidae *anthology call and wrote this over three days. My husband read it and thought the ending needed work. "Pshaw," I said and sent it in. Editor Rhonda Parrish accepted the story, but said the ending needed work. So, I fixed the ending. They were both right. Also, for those keeping track, this is the second story about Hanna the smuggler featured in this collection—a story from early in her career.*

FLYING THE COOP

The man's shoulder, back, and upper arm were coated with bird shit. The responsible party perched on his shoulder, and Hanna eyed it with distaste.

"So let me get this straight. You want me to smuggle that *bird* out of the city?" She couldn't quite keep the horror out of her voice.

The man—Hanna didn't know his name, but inwardly tagged him "Droppings"—frowned. "Not *bird*. Her name is Jenny." He stroked the bird's head. "And, yes, I need you to take her out of the city. Tomorrow. Early."

"Huh." Hanna grabbed a handful of complimentary nuts and dried fruit from the bowl on the table. Jobs had been few and far between for the last few weeks; she was down to one meal a day. "Tomorrow? What's so urgent?"

Droppings shrugged. Lopsidedly. "I can't care for her much longer. The neighbours complain." His face twisted a little, as if he might say more, but he just shrugged again.

"Right." Hanna leaned forward and adjusted the knob of the gaslight lamp, brightening the alcove where they sat. "Let me see her up close."

He lowered the bird to the table, and she hesitated, then stepped down, wings held aloft for balance, croaking irritably.

Jenny was mostly black and white, with streaks of blue on her wings and tail—a magpie. One of her legs was artificial, brass, by the look of it, with miniscule gears and cogs serving as joints. One eye was also clockwork. It *click-clack*ed and a telescopic lens protruded from the socket.

Droppings chuckled. "She's giving you a bit of the same. There's my Jenny."

Hanna pursed her lips. Someone had sunk a lot of money into the bird. Someone with money to waste. How long would a bird like this live? A handful of years?

"Okay," she said, "say I'm interested. There aren't any laws about birds leaving Cisco. Why do you need me?"

"Ha. Well," Droppings said, shifting in his seat, "that has to do with whom Jenny belongs to according to the law."

"She's stolen then?"

The magpie hopped sideways, her brass leg plunking against the wooden surface. She muttered a few syllables, then squawked.

"It's more like she's . . . left. Wants to go someplace else."

Hanna stared at the bird. A runaway pet. Hanna ate another handful of nuts. After a few moments she said, "I'll bite. Where does she want to go?"

"Not far." Droppings smiled. "Just outside the city walls. Someone will meet you."

Hanna's guts churned. She'd heard that before. "Nope. So you can say I delivered her to the wrong person and not pay me?" She pushed away from the table, started to stand.

Jenny squawked and flapped her wings.

"I'll pay in advance."

A crouch was an undignified position to be in for long, so Hanna sat again. "All right. A couple more things before we hash out the nitty-gritty: if she's just going outside the city, why doesn't she go herself? And who is her owner?"

Droppings smiled sadly, echoing the magpie's low croak. "Jenny can no longer fly, due to the augmentations."

Hanna nodded. It was what she'd guessed, but it was good to know these little details. The success of the operation could depend on it. "The owner?" she prodded.

Droppings heaved a sigh. "Tobias Kingsman."

Kingsman! A frisson of excitement swept over Hanna. Pulling a fast one by Kingsman would be a coup.

"The inventor?" she asked.

"And wizard."

Hanna snorted. *Of course,* the man covered in bird shit believed in magic. And, if she were honest, so did many people, people she respected.

She sucked on a nut, considering. High risk, but she needed a job. Pulling off this job would guarantee future jobs. No more bar nuts for dinner.

"I'll do it."

"Thank you," Droppings said, and the bird cawed in agreement. Droppings gestured to Jenny. "I'll leave you two then."

Hanna shook her head. "You were followed," she said flatly. "There is no way Kingsman doesn't know where you are." *Complaining neighbour,* she thought sourly. *Ha. No wonder the bird needs to leave right away.*

"Then you must take her! She's not safe with me!"

"Can't take her yet." She jabbed a finger at the back of the saloon. "Go out through the kitchen—tell Cookie you need the Hanna Express Exit. Then go flop somewhere. A whorehouse. A drug den. Just not your place. Or your friends' Kingsman'll have them watched. Meet me tomorrow morning in Victory Square. And I need that payment now. Got it?"

Jenny the magpie nodded. "Goooddid."

Hanna watched man and bird disappear into the kitchen. She dumped the remaining nuts and dried fruit from the bowl into her oilskin bag—she was still hungry—and tucked the bowl under her duster, trapping it between her arm and ribcage.

Checking her hand-cannons, Hanna left the saloon, the new pouch of coins in her vest jingling. Gaslight lampposts stood on the street corners, casting golden pools of light on the ground. The lamps didn't illuminate much beyond the sidewalks; their light couldn't penetrate the thick night that cloaked the buildings and streets. She hadn't walked ten feet before two shadows detached from the saloon and stepped in front of her.

"What do you have there?" asked one shadow.

"Looks like a birdcage," said the other.

"It's not," Hanna said truthfully. "So how about you let me pass?"

The first shadow chuckled and stepped closer. "Sorry, no can do. A valuable bird was stolen from my boss, and we have reason to believe that you have it."

Hanna wrinkled her nose. "Birds are noisy and dirty. Your boss is welcome to them. Excuse me." She took two quick steps forward and started to brush past the man.

"No you don't!" He grabbed her arm.

The second man closed the distance between them. Hanna snagged the bowl under her duster and threw it at him like a flying disc, then she drew her hand-cannon and shoved it into the stomach of the man holding her arm.

"Now, then," she said and the *click* of her hand-cannon's hammer sounded impossibly loud in the still night air. "I'm going to take my bowl and go home."

The man released her arm. "You're playing smart. Kingsman doesn't like smart. You know what he does to smart girls?"

Hanna did. Broken bones, amputations, burns, and other disfiguring acts of retribution.

Hanna grimaced. Maybe eating nuts for dinner wasn't so bad after all.

She risked a glance at the second man. The bowl had hit true—he sat on the ground with hands cupping his nose. The smear of blood on his mouth and chin looked black in the dim gaslight.

"I'm not playing smart," she sneered. "I *am* smart." Hanna kept her hand-cannon trained on the man as she stooped, picked up the bowl, and backed away. Once she left the gaslamp's nimbus, she let the dark swallow her and ran.

She had to stop at the Opera House before finding a place to bunk for the night, but she had to lose Kingsman's thugs first. She would see them again, when she was ready. If Kingsman was so concerned about the bird leaving the city, tomorrow morning he would be right where Hanna wanted him to be—providing that Droppings and Jenny had escaped the saloon successfully. The job could be over already, but she wouldn't know until tomorrow morning in Victory Square.

Victory Square was large and crowded, even this early. Maybe especially this early, since dozens of food vendors were out with their carts, catching the breakfast rush.

Hanna pushed her way to the fountain that dominated the centre of the square. Finding an empty spot on the rim, she sat down, yawning. She had not slept well, too anxious about Droppings and Jenny. What if they hadn't found a safe place last night?

Yawning again, Hanna adjusted the angle of her flat-brimmed hat so that she wouldn't have to squint against the morning sun, which peeked above the main gate of the city. Guards stood to either side of the opening, and more were stationed in the towers that braced the gates. Hanna caught sight of Droppings, the magpie perched on his shoulder, and grinned. Two men, one of whom was Tobias Kingsman, materialized out of the crowd and fell into step behind Droppings. Kingsman's leonine hair and beard gleamed in the early morning light.

Hanna smirked.

She stood, brushing her braid off her shoulder, as Droppings approached. "Give me the bird and get out of my way," she hissed.

Droppings blinked at her, red-rimmed, sunken eyes testifying to a sleepless night. Jenny muttered anxiously, shuffling from foot to peg and back again.

Kingsman and his goon increased their pace.

"Now, dammit!"

Jenny stepped onto her finger, and Hanna transferred the bird to her left shoulder.

As the magpie settled herself, two things happened.

Tobias Kingsman shouted, "Stop! Thief!", and dozens of women in brown dusters, with magpies on their shoulders and braids thumping against their backs, surrounded Hanna. Their flat-brimmed hats all had red ribbons wrapped around the crowns, just like hers.

Hanna grinned. Renting all the costumes and stuffed birds from the opera company had been expensive, but worth it.

"Hold on, Jenny!" Hanna yelled. She and the pack of imposter Hannas broke into a run, spreading out in all directions. She heard a few women get stopped—guards or concerned citizens, she didn't know—heard shouts and grunts as people were bowled over. Hanna shoved people out of her way and kept her gaze on the gate, ignoring the tiny stings of pain in her shoulder from Jenny's claws. The bird cawed wildly, and Hanna felt another, sharper, pain as the magpie clutched a hank of Hanna's hair with her beak.

The gate guards had pulled out their hand-cannons. That didn't concern her too much; they couldn't risk hitting the crowds of people in the square, but she *was* worried about the heavy gates slowly swinging shut. Hanna burst forward, distancing herself from the handful of Hannas that had run with her to the gate—making herself a target.

Something whizzed by her ear. Another something hit her in the back. She stumbled, almost fell, but kept going, thrusting herself through the gates.

Hanna fell forward into dirt, vaguely aware of the thud as the gates closed. It would take a few minutes for them to reopen the gates, which would hopefully be enough time to rendezvous with Jenny's friend.

"'Orry," the magpie croaked.

Hanna felt the bird leave her shoulder, walk down her back. A glassy pain as something was pulled out of her skin, a crunch as that same something was crushed in Jenny's beak.

Jenny hopped back onto Hanna's shoulder and dropped a metallic blob in the dirt next to Hanna's head. Hanna focused a bleary eye on it. A clockwork bug of some sort . . . ah, she'd heard of Kingsman's bees. Their stingers contained a narcotic, which explained the numbness creeping through her body.

The shrubs that bordered the wide road leading to the gates of the city rustled, and a half-dozen wolves emerged from the thicket.

Behind Hanna, the gates creaked ominously.

Jenny cawed in despair and launched herself from Hanna's shoulder. Flapping her wings did little to slow her descent, and she landed in an ungainly heap on the ground. One of the wolves, a large male with only one eye, dashed forward, scooped the bird into his mouth, and darted back into the protection of the bushes. The other wolves also disappeared.

"Thief! Halt!"

"Hell," Hanna muttered, pushing herself into a kneeling position.

A sword tip pricked the nape of her neck. "Don't move," ordered a guard softly. She spied a second guard from the corner of her eye; he yanked her hand-cannons out of their holsters.

A third person came to stand in front of her. Hanna looked up into the angry face of Tobias Kingsman.

"Where's my bird, thief?" he asked.

"Took off with a wolf."

He flinched. That was interesting.

After a few seconds, Kingsman said, "Nonsense." He squatted, so their eyes were level. "I'll have the guards beat the truth out of you."

Hanna started to shrug, stopped when the sword point at her neck dug deeper. "Yeah, you like punishing people. Tell me something new."

Kingsman *tsk*ed. Standing, he inclined his head. The guard to the right of Hanna kicked her in the gut. She folded as the air whooshed out of her. Coughing and wheezing, she struggled to regain her breath, thankful for the guards. He might not disfigure her while they were present.

She stilled. Kingsman liked to maim people who crossed him. *You know what he does to smart girls?* the thug had asked. *Wizard,* whispered Droppings' voice.

Hanna spat into the dirt and straightened. "You bastard. You did that to Jenny. She used to be a person!" *What are the odds that a one-eyed magpie meets up with a one-eyed wolf?* "And that wolf—who was he?"

"Sir?" asked one of the guards.

"She's delusional," Kingsman scoffed. "Probably the narcotic from my clockwork bee."

"Sir!" an urgent cry of distress.

The sharp pressure against her neck suddenly withdrew, and Hanna crawled away from the guards, her sluggish body collapsing after a couple of feet. Then she discovered what had startled her captors.

The wolves had returned. Jenny sat on the shoulder of the one-eyed male.

After exchanging glances with his partner, one of the guards said, "If she told the truth about the wolf, what else was she right about?"

"Kiiiing," croaked Jenny.

"It talks!" said the guard with the sword. The second guard, the one with Hanna's hand-cannons, raised the weapons and pointed them at Kingsman.

Kingsman reached into his pocket, muttering, his face tight with anger.

"Magic!" Hanna yelled. "Gag him!"

Hand-cannon guard fired. Kingsman yelped and fell to the ground. Blood oozed from one foot. Sword guard stuffed a cloth in Kingsman's mouth, jerked his arms behind his back, and handcuffed him.

"I'll go find the captain," sword guard said. He trotted to the gates. Hand-cannon guard kept his weapons trained on Kingsman.

"Pesky things, aren't they, those laws against forced augmentations?" Hanna yearned to kick Kingsman while she had a chance, but her drug-heavy limbs couldn't even twitch. She'd settle for needling him. "Think the judge will stretch them to cover transfiguration?"

The one-eyed wolf yipped, and Jenny cackled with amusement.

Hand-cannon guard abruptly dropped one weapon and rummaged in his pouch, bringing out a sketch pad and a piece of charcoal. He scribbled on the pad, glancing at Jenny and the wolves every few seconds.

Sword guard was returning, with a few other guards, one of whom wore a much fancier hat—the captain, Hanna assumed—and . . . Droppings. Hanna allowed herself a smile. Kingsman wouldn't be able to wriggle out of this quagmire, not with Droppings' testimony on top of the guards' tale.

Jenny cawed, drawing everyone's attention. The newcomers halted and stared at her.

The magpie bowed. She lifted one wing and waved it at Hanna; awkwardly turned and waved at Droppings. She cawed again, and the wolves retreated into the bushes, vanishing.

Kingsman spat out his gag and glared at Hanna. "You think you've won, little thief?" he snarled. "Just remember this: the spell can't be undone. You can't save Jenny. Her brother can't save Jenny. She and her miserable lover will live out their days as beasts. They will *never* forget me."

The city guards pulled Kingsman to his feet. "You shouldn't forget me either," he said before they escorted him to the guard station. "Enjoy your reputation, little thief."

Hanna sighed. He was right: her reputation was made. She would be one of the most sought-after smugglers in the area. She could raise her fees, live a little better. And Jenny and the one-eyed wolf, her once-human lover, would spend the rest of their lives as animals. Jenny would never see her family, her brother Droppings, again.

Hanna's success tasted bitter.

SUNDERED

Originally published as "X" in *G is for Ghosts*, edited by Rhonda Parrish. Poise and Pen Publishing, 2021.

I was thrilled to be invited to contribute to one of Rhonda Parrish's Alphabet anthologies. I was assigned the letter X and knew immediately that X-ray would be the topic—frankly, I was amazed it hadn't been used in previous entries of the Alphabet series. Further inspiration came courtesy of my husband, a physicist, who often regales us with the stories behind the discoveries. Wilhelm Röntgen took an X-ray of his wife Anna Bertha's hand, and she apparently did exclaim, "This is my death!" upon seeing the film.

SUNDERED

asting disease is what they call it. The nurses cluck as they arrange blankets around the pale husk of my body, composing a peaceful scene for Wilhelm.

Am I dead? I don't feel so, and I can see my body breathing, shallowly and slowly. But death seems not far off, from the downcast expressions of the nurses. I try to explain that I'm *fine*, but they don't see my waves or hear my cries for attention. Frustrated, I pull my mouth into a frightful grimace and shout at them. They don't react.

When they turn for the door, I leap after them, and that is when I discover that my *self*, my spark, has separated from my physical form. Confused, I stare down at my ghostly body, as wispy as a cloud, and then at the bed, where my solid body breathes. The experience is so unnerving that I stay in place, uncertain what I should do. The nurses leave without looking back.

Eventually, Wilhelm arrives and carefully sits at my bedside, clasping one of my husk's hands. He looks tired, eyes rimmed red and bloodshot. I wish to console him, to explain that I'm simply unrooted from my earthly body, but like the nurses, Wilhelm doesn't hear me. My hands pass through his shoulders. He shivers a little and glances toward the window.

My hands. They are transparent, as is, I discover, my entire body. It is horrifying, yet I am relieved that while I can see through myself, I cannot see beneath the skin like Wilhelm's dread machine. Fear fills me at the memory of the invention.

"I am ready, Bertha. Please keep still."

Buzzing. A green glow.

I moan and the walls of my bedroom dissolve into white mist.

When I return to myself, I am not in my bedroom, but Wilhelm's laboratory.

Skinny black bones.

More mist.

I am still in the laboratory. It's very quiet; Wilhelm isn't here. Is he still with my earthly body, in my bedroom? The familiar white mist creeps into my vision, but I focus on my feet. I will not fade out again.

"He's at my bedside," I say, the sound of my voice bolstering my courage. I risk quick glances around the laboratory. The high windows, the heavy blinds drawn aside. The bare wooden floors. The large clock dominating the wall over the many tables crammed with scientific equipment. I try to resist the long table in the middle of the room, but I cannot ignore it.

The machine spreads across the table like mould: the wires, the huge cylindrical electricity generator, and the glass tube hanging from a metal rod. The rod is anchored by a metal box meant for holding photographic plates. A chair sits at the end of the table, close to the plate box and the dangling bulb—the Crookes tube, as Wilhelm calls it.

Despite the colour leeching from my vision, I drift to the chair. My hand hovers over the plate box.

"Nothing to worry about, Bertha," Wilhelm said calmly as he adjusted the tear drop-shaped glass tube hanging over her hand. "I've run the experiment several times."

But not with a person, she thought, immediately feeling guilty for doubting him. They'd been married twenty-three years, and Wilhelm was attentive and devoted. They had a daughter. He would never harm her.

"Yes, Wilhelm," she said aloud, her voice squeaking. Her right hand, her free hand, bunched the heavy fabric of her dress.

The laboratory was dimly lit, the curtains drawn shut, so
Wilhelm could run the experiment properly. She was certain he
could not see the tightness of her clenched jaw. All he noticed
was the relaxed hand resting on the photographic plate.

I retreat from the table and the equipment it holds. It is
pointless to be near the machine and revisit disturbing
memories—memories that make me ill. I shouldn't be here. I
should be with Wilhelm. He will have sent for Josephine, and I
don't want to miss what could be my last sight of my daughter. I
turn from the machine and rush to the door. But at the door, I am
stopped. My transparent hands cannot grasp the door knob. Yet
they are too solid to pass through the door.

"No!" I shout, and pound at the door with my fists. It is utterly
silent, the only sound my panicked gulps of air, not quite sobs. "I
will not stay here!"

My pleas are unheeded, and after interminable moments, I
sink to the floor.

I am trapped with the machine.

Awareness recedes and returns as I sob dryly into my hands.
Eventually, my shoulders cease shaking and my sobs fade. With
one last shuddering sigh, I raise my head and stare blankly at the
door. I can hear faint sounds of household activity. The maids, no
doubt, going about their routine.

The distant noise is comforting. I am not alone. Tentatively, I
reach out to the door and once again meet with resistance. Alone,
yet not alone.

I am here because of that cursed machine. I force myself to
stand and glare at the contraption. A sudden flood of anger
propels me forward, and I swing a hand at the glass tube.

Ting!

I flinch, startled. I had touched it! My hand falls to my side,
and now I am ashamed. The machine is important to Wilhelm.
Damaging it would hurt him.

Wilhelm had been so excited about the new discovery.
Something unexpected had happened while he was running his
cathode ray experiment. A new ray, he'd explained over supper.
Invisible light.

He'd asked me to help, since he was testing which substances
could and could not block the new rays. I sigh, as the rest of the

memory comes back to me.

Wilhelm fiddled with the placement of the Crookes tube again, and she realized he was nervous.

Finally, he said, "I am ready, Bertha. Please keep still."

He smiled a little as he returned to the table. A flip of a lever and the electricity generator hummed to life. A green glow emitted from several items in the laboratory.

After a few seconds, the light faded and the generator's buzz quieted.

Wilhelm lifted her hand from the plate and she let it flop into her lap. He grinned and held up the photographic plate in front of her. "Look, Bertha!"

The glass clearly showed a hand, but not the plump pink appendage that she was familiar with. The glass showed bones. Skinny black bones.

She almost scoffed and teased Wilhelm for creating a fake photograph, but then she noticed the dark band circling one finger. Her wedding ring.

"My death!" she gasped, feeling lightheaded. "This is my death, Wilhelm."

The reminder of what happens to all human beings had unnerved me. Death reduces us to bones and dust. But I'm not dead now, am I? Just . . . sundered. Adrift. My hands run over the machine. The generator. The plate box. I even try to touch the delicate Crookes tube, from which the mysterious x-rays emit, but there is no indication that I make physical contact.

The machine has been a source of terror, and I am now convinced it is the source of my grief. However, my hands can't manipulate the generator, the source of the electricity needed to trigger the x-ray creation. Wilhelm can, though. I just need to make him understand.

I skim to the door again, filled with purpose and determination, and I pass through the door unimpeded.

Wilhelm sits by my bed, cradling one of my hands between his, head bowed.

I glide to his side. He had sensed my presence earlier, had felt the chill of my movements. He has to, again. Or my earthly body will die, and my spirit with it.

I stroke his head. I cannot feel his hair, but a few strands stir. His shoulders hunch, and he looks up.

I gasp. He *can* feel me, even if he can't see me! I lean close to him and whisper, "Wilhelm," directly into his ear.

He cries out and jumps to his feet. And then he asks, "Who's there?"

I feel unbearably light with joy, and the world becomes tinged with white. I mustn't fade, so I focus on my husband's sturdy figure, his sunken, intense eyes, his bushy black beard streaked with grey.

He will understand! I laugh giddily and run my hand down his cheek and tug his beard. It is a familiar, affectionate gesture.

He shivers. "Bertha?" he asks. He glances to the bed, where my body lies, and frowns.

"I'm here, Wilhelm," I say, and tug his beard again.

He raises one hand slowly, almost dreamily, and strokes his chin. "Bertha," he says firmly. "I don't understand. How . . . ?"

"I don't know, my love," I say. And I don't, not the mechanics. I'm no scientist. But I know that the machine holds the solution to my terrible separation of selves. Always the machine.

Desperate, I push my body's left hand. It twitches. Wilhelm, sharp-eyed as ever, grasps the hand and runs his fingers over my limp digits—and my wedding ring. His fingers pause on the simple gold band, and he takes a deep breath.

"The x-rays, Bertha? Are they what have stolen you from me?"

I tweak his beard again.

"I will fix this," he declares, his gaze roving the room. "I promise."

I caress his cheek one more time, before the fog overtakes me.

The repeated use of my name pulls me from the void. It takes several moments for the fog to clear, and I fear that whatever thin tether that ties me here will soon break and my body truly will die.

My bed and body have been moved to Wilhelm's laboratory. My left hand rests on the photographic plate, and Wilhelm bustles around the machine, teasing the equipment into place. He explains the procedure while he works, a stream of words peppered with my name. I have difficulty hearing all the words, his voice very faint, and I become concerned that my time grows short. Wilhelm's theory must prove correct.

The theory is simple enough that I follow the idea even though I don't understand the underlying physics.

"So, Bertha, I will need both of your hands on the plate glass," he says, while adjusting the bulbs. "I have here your earthly hand, but I also need your . . . spectral hand. Here, like so." He gently places his hand over the hand of my husk. "I will take the x-ray radiograph, and God willing, your two states will be fused once more."

His gaze flits around the room, eyes a little wild. To reassure him of my presence, I wave my hand over his hair. His skin breaks into gooseflesh from the chill, but he smiles.

"Ah, good, you understand," he says. "You stay here, and I will start the experiment."

I place my left hand on top of my husk's hand. The wedding bands should have clinked, my two hands line up so perfectly. I avoid looking at my husk. The waxy skin and slow, shallow breathing disturb me. My husk is more dead than alive.

"Bertha, I'm going to turn on the machine. Are you ready?"

"Yes," I say, although my voice is nothing but a whisper on a breeze, but he senses my response. Wilhelm nods and flips the lever.

The machine hums, and I imagine the tubes crackling with energy. The familiar green glow suffuses the room, the radiation reacting with Wilhelm's fluorescent materials.

Skinny black bones.

I blanch and my hand twitches, but I don't remove it. As the green glow diminishes and the buzzing generator quiets, the laboratory sinks into darkness. I wait for Wilhelm to turn on the lights, to remove my hand from the photographic plate, but he doesn't appear.

"Wilhelm?" I call, but my voice isn't working.

The additional radiation experiment has failed, and I am dying. I sob, or try, but nothing works. My phantasmal body no longer mimics my earthly one.

"Bertha?"

Wilhelm's voice is muffled. Is he in a different room? I must reassure him that I am still here, even if his experiment failed.

We must try again.

My eyes flutter open and Wilhelm's dear face fills my field of vision. He smiles, but his eyes are glassy with tears.

I am hungry. I am exhausted. I am bewildered.

"Wilhelm?" I ask, my voice dry and dusty.

"Bertha." He beams.

I am alive, I wonder, and raise my arms off the bed. I pinch my left hand, twirl my wedding ring around my finger. I am solid. It worked! The machine has made me whole once more.

"Wilhelm," I cry again and embrace my husband, relishing the sturdiness of his body.

THE COACH GIRL

Originally published in *Clockwork, Curses, and Coal*, edited by Rhonda Parrish. World Weaver Press, 2021.

I had been poking at an adaptation of the Grimms' tale "The Goose Girl" for a while when World Weaver Press posted their call for steampunk fairy tales. It was the impetus I needed to finish the story, integrating steampunk elements. I am quite fond of the character Percolator, who was inspired by the Toaster in Red Dwarf, *and I was thrilled to give Falada a happy ending (I was traumatized as a child by Falada's death in a PBS adaptation of the original fairy tale).*

THE COACH GIRL

Tara upended her canteen into her mouth and was rewarded with a single drop of warm water. The stories about The Crossing had not prepared her for the reality. It was dry. It was dusty. Her hands resembled snakeskin, fine diamond patterns etched on her skin. She couldn't ration her water, gulping it down as soon as her flask was filled. She had never been so thirsty in her entire life.

Maybe she should request a stop; after all, they'd been on the road since breakfast—the driver could probably do with a rest, too. Tara grabbed her walking stick, raised the knob towards the roof of the coach, and hesitated. Sienna, the driver, wasn't the most pleasant person. Maybe Tara could wait a while longer.

Her nose twitched. Tara peeled back the curtain. An oasis! Not an inhabited one, unfortunately, because she would have enjoyed warm food and pleasant company, but there would be fresh water. Her tongue seemed to swell at the thought. Tara rapped the coach roof.

After a moment, the hatch slid open. "What?"

"Sienna, I noticed that we're passing an oasis. Could we stop?"

Sienna huffed. "Did you drink all your water again?"

Tara's face warmed. She considered retracting her request out of sheer embarrassment, but changed her mind again. "Yes."

"Cripes." The hatch slammed shut.

Steam hissed and burbled through pipes as the coach veered towards the oasis. The land was rougher here, and Tara was jostled against the wall.

Soon the coach wheezed to a halt. After a few scrapes from above, the coach dipped and rose with Sienna's departure. Tara waited for the door to open, and when it became clear that it wasn't going to, she fumbled with the latch.

She gave up in seconds. "Sienna? I can't open the door, could you help me?"

The door swung open with a squeal. "This damn dust," Sienna said, peering at the hinges, voice muffled by the bandana that covered her lower face. "I'll have to oil those again, or you won't be able to get out at all." She tugged down her bandana, revealing a wide smile. For a moment she resembled a shark. Tara shivered.

Sienna pressed a button, and the coach whirred and clanked. Stairs unfolded from a slot beneath the door. Grasping the jamb, Tara descended the steps. It was tricky, because of the dress she wore. It took nearly a minute. She gazed at the smudge of water and calculated how many tiny steps it would take to reach it. Desperately, she held her flask out to Sienna.

The driver blinked, and a vein in her temple pulsed. "I've got to oil that door and restock the burner." Sienna jabbed a finger at each object in turn, shook her head, and climbed back on top of the coach, where the tool kit was kept.

Tara glanced down at her canteen, tears pricking her eyes. Her dress, while the height of fashion in Dunston, was impractical for a journey like the Crossing. It cinched in tightly at the knees, limiting her movement. With small, hesitant steps, she walked to the water. It was a marsh, she noticed with surprise. The last oasis had been a charming spring, where a couple ran a government way station and fruit tree orchard.

Cattails and lizard tails grew along the edge of and within the shallow water; a few shrubby willows provided some shade. Tara crouched awkwardly and plunged her canteen into the water. Bubbles rose to the surface with a satisfying gurgle. "Ha! Nothing to it." A pleased smile lightened her face, until it occurred to her that she would now have to stand up in her blasted dress.

She scowled and peeked over her shoulder at Sienna. Why

hadn't Mama sent one of the servants along on this trip? Someone to help with her clothing? "And it would be nice to have a familiar face in my new home," she admitted aloud, quietly, to her canteen.

Tara drained the flask in a few unladylike gulps, then re-filled it, smiling again at the sound of burbling water, the sound of her success. She pulled out a handkerchief that was discreetly tucked into her bodice. It was plain white, of a cheap fabric, with one knotted corner. Her mama had given it to her as they had said their goodbyes, so Tara kept it close. Her mama was a formidable magic user and there was no telling what was stored in that knot. Tara dampened the handkerchief and patted at her face, throat, behind her ears, and the nape of her neck. She felt a little cooler.

She'd delayed standing for as long as possible. Spreading her feet apart as wide as she could, Tara rocked back on her heels and pushed upward, arms stretched in front of her. She felt silly, and knew she must have looked sillier, but she managed to get upright without falling. With mincing steps, she returned to the coach.

Tara eyed the stairs and sighed. Some of the steam coaches in Dunston had installed lifts to accommodate the hobble fashion raging through women's wear, but this coach spent little time in the city. Steam gurgled in the pipes, sounding almost apologetic. Grasping the handle, Tara prepared to hop on the steps, since it was nigh impossible to climb them normally.

"What're you doing?" Sienna asked. Her driving goggles, bandana, and flat-brimmed hat rested in a small heap on the ground.

"I'm getting back into the coach?" Tara cringed at the questioning lilt. "Don't we need to get started?"

"Oh, yeah, but a few minutes more won't make much difference. We'll make Sweetgrass tonight," Sienna said. She drew her hand cannon from its holster. "C'mon, step away from the coach or I'll shoot."

"I . . . don't understand."

"Look, sister, you got two choices: step out here next to me, or be forcibly dragged to this spot after I shoot you. Understand now?"

Tara's lips quivered. She bit down on the lower one to keep

from crying as she complied with Sienna's order. Her eyes remained focused on the hand cannon.

Sienna nodded. "Wasn't so bad, was it? Now take off the dress."

"I won't!" Tara blushed.

The muzzle of the hand cannon dipped and the weapon coughed. The sand at Tara's feet spurted outwards and upwards. Tara screamed and her fingers flew to the column of tiny buttons on her back.

She struggled with the dress for several minutes before it slid off, leaving her in her silk corset and muslin bloomers. Although it was midday in the desert, Tara shivered and hugged herself. "Why are you doing this?"

Sienna grinned. She started to take off her own clothes with one hand; the hand cannon never wavered from its target. "You're selling yourself, aren't you, marrying some cattle baron that you've never met? What good are you going to do him, other than give him money? Help me into that dress, will you?"

Tara picked up her dress and took it to Sienna. With shaking fingers, she guided the dress over Sienna's head, pushed arms through sleeves, and started doing up buttons.

"The way I figure it, *you* have nothing of practical use to bring to the partnership, but I do. Besides, I'm tired of hauling you hoity-toity types back and forth across the Expanse." Sienna stepped away from Tara and admired the dress. "Very nice. A suitable outfit to meet my new husband."

Tara curled her hands into fists, ignoring the small pain caused by her nails digging into her palms. Her mama would have a fit if she knew about this. An image rose in her mind, one of her mama unloosing a knot and releasing a wind. Tara smiled. A charm would teach Sienna a lesson.

"You'll apologize for this insult," Tara said. She whipped out the handkerchief tucked into her bosom and tugged at the knot.

"What're you going to do? Flog me with that tissue?" Sienna laughed long and loud. Tears of mirth trickled from the corner of her eyes.

Tara hunched her shoulders. Her whole body trembled with fear. "B-blow, little wind, b-blow some sense into S-Sienna." She plucked at the knot, but the wet fabric refused to come undone.

"Please?" she whispered.

"Well," Sienna said, wiping her eyes, "we really need to head out. So, put away your hankie, put on my old clothes, and I'll boost you onto the driver's bench." The hand cannon pointed the way.

Tara did as she was bid, her cheeks turning red and blotchy from her drippy nose and the tears streaming down her face. Not even the sounds of Sienna cursing at the useless dress which prevented her from walking properly could keep Tara's tears from falling. At last, she placed a booted foot into Sienna's linked hands, and the woman pushed Tara up into the driver's spot.

"I've pre-programmed the coach," Sienna said. "All you got to do is push that green button and look smart—think you can do that?"

After suffering so many indignities, Tara couldn't muster any feeling about the slight against her intelligence. She nodded.

"Good. I'll get inside then." Sienna cocked her head. "Before I forget . . . Tara, if you tell anybody about what happened here, I'll kill you. Got it?" She patted the butt of her hand cannon, flat black eyes watching Tara with impersonal curiosity. Tara was reminded again of the sharks in the city aquarium.

Tara nodded again, a wave of revulsion rippling over her skin.

She sat with her hands folded in her lap, waiting for Sienna to signal that she was seated. When the rap sounded, Tara flinched, but leaned forward and pressed the green button. The coach gurgled and coughed. Tara patted the box. "If I can do this, you can do this," she said. As if it understood, the coach rumbled and stuttered forward a few feet before finding its rhythm. It trundled through the desert, steam percolating through pipes and tanks with contented hisses.

Tara clutched the edges of her bench, eyes squeezed shut. Sitting up so high, without the security of four walls and a ceiling, made her stomach roil. She hoped that nothing crossed the path of the coach, because she wouldn't see it and halt the coach in time to prevent a collision.

She moaned softly for many minutes until the sudden inhalation of a bug forced her to clamp her mouth shut. The acrid taste of the insect lingered on her tongue for a long time.

Eventually Tara cracked open her eyes, peering at the passing desert landscape. It wasn't as monochromatic as she had thought, with variations of yellow, brown, and even green giving the land a harsh beauty. The rhythmic sway of the coach lulled her into a light doze.

Sharp knocks on the coach roof woke Tara. The sun hung low over the horizon and the barest traces of pink and purple lined the sky.

Sienna yelled from the coach's interior, "We're almost there. Look smart!"

Tara straightened. Shading her face with her hand, she squinted. Sure enough, she could just make out a neat row of buildings. A town. Sweetgrass. She gulped. Her mama had surely sent pictures of Tara, hadn't she? Who would get married without at least seeing a picture of the prospective spouse? Other than herself. Tara wouldn't recognize her intended groom, Thomas Fairbanks, if her life depended on it. Remembering the hand cannon in Sienna's unwavering grip, Tara gulped again. It did.

Sienna hollered instructions on how to slow and stop the coach as it rolled into the town. Tara yanked on the black lever, slammed the red button, and lurched forward as the coach jerked to a stop. "Sorry!" Tara whispered. The pipes moaned, something clunked, and then the steam engine sputtered and died with a whine. Tara winced. The coach sounded like she felt: tired, worn out, and beaten down.

A group of people approached the coach, stopping a few feet from the coach door. After several seconds, Tara realized that they weren't there to help her down. She wasn't a lady here; she was the coach driver. Clutching the railing, she swung one leg, then the other, out of the box. Her toes scrabbled to find a perch, and then her arms began to shake. Her grip loosened, and she fell onto the ground.

Tara stared at the purpling sky, aware of a low buzzing that gradually separated into words. A pair of hands grabbed her shoulders. "Are you all right, miss?"

Tara coughed. "Y-yes."

The hands pulled her to her feet. Tara looked up into a lined face with hound dog eyes.

"I didn't know you needed help, Miss . . . ?" he asked.

Tara coughed again. She couldn't seem to get enough air into her lungs, and her limbs felt far away from her body. "It's been a long day."

"Sienna!" called the duplicitous driver from within the coach. "What happened?"

"Oh." Tara turned her head. "That's . . . I need to help her out."

She trudged to the coach and pushed the button that she had seen Sienna use. The steps whirred as they unfolded. Tara yanked on the door handle, and it opened smoothly. Sienna must have oiled it earlier.

Sienna slid-stepped down the stairs, muttering about the hobble dress, and shoved Tara out of the way. Her frizzy hair had been tamed into a smooth knot at the back of her head, and the travel grime had been cleaned from her face and hands. Tara gasped and raised her own hands to her face. Even if Thomas had been sent a photograph of her, he wouldn't recognize her. Sienna hadn't given Tara the goggles, bandana, or hat, and Tara had no doubt that her face was caked with dirt and bug guts.

"Tara!" The man with hound dog eyes walked to Sienna and clasped her hands. "I'm Jack Fairbanks. I'm pleased to meet you. Here's my son, Thomas." Jack waved a hand, and another, younger, man stepped out from the small group.

Thomas bent over Sienna's hand and brushed it with his lips. He murmured some pleasantry that Tara couldn't hear. Then he tucked Sienna's arm around his own and led her away.

Tara was left alone in the dying sunlight.

Hot tears flowed from her eyes. So much for Thomas Fairbanks coming to her rescue. Tara sat on the folding steps of the coach, buried her face in her hands, and sobbed.

A polite cough alerted her to the presence of another person. She swallowed a sob and looked up, scrubbing at her face. A boy stood there, fidgeting.

"Uh, I'm supposed to bring Miss Tara's bags," he said. "What's wrong with you?"

Tara smiled at his bluntness. "I've never driven a coach before, and I don't know what to do with it now."

The boy's eyes widened, the whites gleaming in the dim light. "You made The Crossing on your first drive? Wow!"

Tara nodded. "And the coach made a funny noise when we pulled into town. I'm not sure it works."

"Huh." The boy scratched his head. "You can leave it for now, and we'll get someone from the livery to take a look tomorrow. I'll take you over to the inn. M'name's London, by the way."

"I'm . . ." Tara hesitated. She didn't want to take Sienna's name, but she couldn't use her own. "Lily." It was her middle name and should be familiar enough that she wouldn't forget it. "London? I don't have any money."

London nodded, as if that were completely normal. "Okay. Help me with Miss Tara's bags, and then I'll get you settled somewhere."

"There's just the one trunk." Tara peered at his gangly body. "I'm not sure—"

"I can carry it!"

Tara shrugged. She didn't want to alienate the only friend she had.

Tara stretched and winced. Her body ached all over. No surprise, really, after the uncomfortable coach ride, her fall, and helping London haul that damnably heavy trunk to the inn, which despite his boasting, proved too much for his small frame. She sat up, brushing hay from her clothes. Sleeping in the barn hadn't helped her body recuperate either, but it was free.

A horse thrust its head over the stall and whickered. "Thanks for the reminder," Tara said, reaching up to stroke the velvet nose. "Not free, but in exchange for work." The barn needed another stable hand.

Tara hadn't seen a living horse in years. She had fond memories of riding them when she was a little girl, but horseless carriages and coaches were all the rage, and the use of horses had dwindled in Dunston.

A couple of hours later she was hot, sweaty, and muttering curses as she shovelled out another stall. Although she wore gloves, her hands burned. Tara didn't believe she could work enough days to earn the money to send a telegram to her mama. Tears rose in her eyes again and she blinked rapidly to dispel them.

She thrust the shovel under a mound of hay and something gushed on her hand. Tara hissed and drew the hand back. A small dark spot dotted the glove. Blood.

She couldn't stop the tears this time. Why couldn't Mama, with all her magic, have foreseen the disasters of this trip? Tara sniffed, the tears drying up. Sienna hadn't wanted Tara's handkerchief; she hadn't understood its significance.

Tara reached into the pocket of her leather vest and withdrew the plain white handkerchief. The cloth was dry. She tugged at the knot. "Blow, little wind, blow," Tara whispered. But the knot did not loosen and the air of the barn remained still.

Tara stuffed the cloth back into her pocket. She needed money. Her hands were blistered and bleeding from unaccustomed labour, and her mama's charmed handkerchief wouldn't work. For a moment, Tara considered walking to the inn, where Sienna stayed, and denouncing her in front of everybody. The daydream played out, the shocked gasps of the guests, the gushing apologies from Thomas, the anger on Sienna's face . . . and then a gunshot and agony. Tara rubbed her stomach, massaging away the phantom pain. No, no exposure yet. Not that way.

A wisp of straw poked through her pants. "Ouch!" Tara plucked the offending stalk from her leg and twirled it. "Stupid straw." She glared at it, bending it easily, wrapping it around her fingers.

"Oh." Tara stared at the twisted straw, then bent and grabbed more from the floor. She looped two stalks around a finger, crossed the ends, and pulled. A knot.

Heart thumping with excitement, Tara grabbed two more stalks of straw. As she tied the knot, she whispered, "I need this barn shovelled, I need this barn shovelled." Her mama had more lyrical, rhyming chants, but all she really needed was intent. Tara tied another knot, repeating the desire for a shovelled barn. Not so much as a single stalk of straw stirred. Tara sighed. She'd never really had the knack of knot magic; her mama had despaired of teaching her. With a sigh, she picked up the shovel.

After a few more awkward and painful stabs at the straw, Tara tossed the shovel aside again. Her eyes lit on the steam coach. Nobody had checked it after it had been hauled to the barn last night. In a town of horses, there was no need for a steam mechanic.

Tara glanced at the work she'd done. More stalls needed

mucking out, but she'd made noticeable progress. With her hurt hand, surely no one would begrudge her a break?

She stowed away the shovel and walked to the steam coach. It was filthy with dirt and sand. A horse would have been groomed after the long trip—why, even she had been allowed a basin of water to clean her face last night. Exploring the coach's storage compartments, Tara found cloths and polish. The polish couldn't go on until the grime had been cleared, so she set to cleaning the coach, pumping a bucket of water from the horses' trough in the paddock.

It was dirty work, and her muscles ached, and more blisters had burst, but the coach finally gleamed in the dimming light of day. It practically buzzed with pleasure as she rubbed a polishing cloth over the control box.

Tara paused. The coach *was* buzzing, no practically about it. And hadn't it seemed to hiss and gurgle in response to her remarks yesterday?

"Hello?" she asked.

The buzzing stopped.

Tara frowned. "I must be lonelier than I thought, talking to a machine. Of course, you weren't buzzing."

The coach's whistle gave an indignant toot.

I am talking to a steam coach, Tara thought. *I've had too much sun, or—or I fainted while shovelling!*

The coach hummed and the whistle moaned. The coach rocked.

Tara's eyes popped open. "Okay, settle down, coach. You're talking to me, I get it." She patted the control box. "Did . . . did you talk to Sienna?"

Disdainful whistle.

That lifted her spirits, although Tara laughed at herself. Imagine being more upset about the coach liking Sienna than her betrothed liking Sienna!

"So, what's your name?" Tara asked. "I can't call you coach."

Air blew gently through the whistle, warm gusts that formed syllables. "Fa-la-da."

"Falada?" Tara repeated. At the coach's affirming toot, Tara smiled. "Nice to meet you, Falada. Now, you're clean, but something broke when we arrived in Sweetgrass. I apologize for hurting you. It was my first time driving, and I didn't know what I was doing. Can you tell me what's wrong?"

Falada's control box thrummed, and then something clanked below.

"Under the passenger box?" Tara guessed.

Falada tooted an affirmative, and Tara clambered gingerly to the ground. The descent was easier this time, now that she was more familiar with the coach. Lighting a lantern, Tara crawled underneath the coach and held aloft the light.

Some pipes had come loose, and a puddle of dirty water stained the ground. Tara reached out and touched one dangling pipe. Air rushed through the tubing, not forming words precisely, but communicating nonetheless. She could *see* how to fix the coach.

Tara was rubbing the soft cloth over Falada's chimney when London burst into the barn.

"Lily, what are you—" He blinked, mouth dropping open. "Wow. You musta worked all day on your coach. But," he tugged her arm, "there's a big to-do at the inn. That fancy lady married the boss's son. They're having a big dinner an' everyone's invited!"

Married already? Tara thought incredulously. She knew that was the purpose of the trip, that marriage had been the arrangement between her mama and Thomas's father, but she'd been expecting some time to become acquainted with her betrothed.

Falada gave a low whistle and Tara nodded. Of course, she wouldn't have needed to rush her wedding—Sienna had stolen Tara's life. A hasty ceremony before her deception was discovered was to her advantage.

Tara must have taken too long with her thoughts because London said, "There's lots of food. Even cake!" When she still didn't answer, he tugged at her arm again. "Come with me, it'll be fun."

Falada blatted, a cloud of soot puffing from its chimney.

London looked at the coach askance. "Is it . . . on?"

"No," Tara said. "Just dirt working its way out. The Crossing was pretty dusty." She placed the polishing cloth on the driver's bench. "All right," she said, patting the coach so that Falada knew it was included in her response, "I'll go to the dinner."

London didn't mention freshening up—and she didn't have any spare clothes anyhow—so she walked to the inn still wearing her grimy shirt and trousers. Tendrils of hair tickled her neck and ears, and she was fairly certain grease smudged her face, given the stains on her hands. Her mama would have had a fit if she knew, and Tara chuckled. For good and ill, her mama was very far away and had no influence on events here in Sweetgrass.

London eagerly pushed through the swinging double doors of the inn. Tara hesitated before following. Even in the dim light of evening, she could see the peeling paint, the dangerously sagging sidewalk boards. The inn, with its restaurant and saloon, was the social heart of the little town, and it was falling apart. Treading carefully on the cracked planking, Tara went through the door.

Everyone in the town must have been there, the room was so full. Tables laden with food lined the walls. Mostly plain, hearty fare: potato dishes, roast beef, several kinds of bread, roasted root vegetables. But there was also a cake, as London had promised, a snowy white, tiered confection which dominated a single table set on the opposite side of the room from the dinner fare. The little folding table sagged under the weight of the enormous dessert.

A beverage station was set up next to the cake table. There were a couple of large punch bowls of some presumably fruity drink and, she was surprised to see, a steam-powered coffee percolator. She smiled. She was oddly fond of percolators and tea kettles—their burbling and chugging always seemed cheerful and never failed to lighten her mood.

Hmmm. Tara tipped her head to one side and considered the percolator. Had they *seemed* cheerful or were they *actually* cheerful? Had she been reading the moods of steam devices all these years and not realized it?

She walked to the table, squeezing between well-dressed women and men and stepping around children. She halted in front of the table and, feeling a little silly, waved to the machine. "Hello, percolator."

The coffee machine gurgled and its power button flashed. It was enormously pleased to see her and asked anxiously if she were thirsty, did she want some coffee, it would be *so honoured* to warm up the brew currently in its canister, as it felt it had grown somewhat tepid in the last hour as most of the human-folk seemed to like that inferior fruit drink—

"I'd love a cup of coffee, thank you, percolator," Tara interrupted. As the percolator hummed in excitement and quivered as its heating element engaged, Tara stared at it in wonder. She could understand steam machines—had for a very long time, probably. She was her mama's daughter, but her gift lay with machinery instead of knots and wind.

She grinned foolishly to herself as the percolator re-heated the coffee and poured a cup out for her. It proudly directed her to a number of sweetening agents, such as pure granulated sugar, imported from a far-away island, and honey, harvested from local hives, and thick cream from the very cows that ate the sweetgrass for which the town was named, and even a fruit syrup, guava it thought, from some oasis that lay—

"Just a little honey, thank you, percolator," Tara said. She patted its beautiful copper lid and turned towards the collection of sweeteners, bumping into a person who was approaching the table.

"I do beg your—" Tara began, then gasped.

Sienna's eyes widened and the laughter which had been spilling from her mouth shrivelled into a discordant jangle. "You," she hissed. "What are you doing here?"

She was wearing Tara's dress, beaded, hand-tatted lace, the highest of fashion in Dunston. Tara smirked at the poor fit. People being people, Sienna's ill-fitting dress would be the talk of the town tomorrow—at least among the women.

Thomas, the man who should have been Tara's husband, stood at Sienna's elbow and looked puzzled. "Aren't you the coach driver girl?" he asked.

Sienna fumbled with her heavy skirts. "I warned you!"

Tara took one moment to feel horrified that Sienna had mutilated the dress to manufacture a pocket for a hand cannon before dropping to the floor. The cup shattered, and her coffee streamed across the floor, splashing the hem of Sienna's dress.

"Tara, what in the world?!" Thomas shouted. He lunged for Sienna's arm, but she had already drawn the hand cannon.

"Percolator!" Tara shouted. "Spray coffee!"

Percolator was overjoyed to provide assistance for its friend, and coffee geysered from its spout, drenching Sienna's torso. She screamed, folding in on herself, but her outstretched hand still clutched the hand cannon.

Tara couldn't reach the hand cannon, but she grabbed the hem of the dress and yanked. Sienna teetered and wind-milled her arms, but in the restrictive hobble-style wedding dress, she couldn't maintain her balance. Sienna fell forward. Tara twisted out of Sienna's path and shoved her aside. Sienna collided heavily with the cake table. The tabletop collapsed and the cake slid onto Sienna's head. The hand cannon clattered to the floor.

Tara was vaguely aware of the din of the crowd, but she was focused too intensely on Sienna and the hand cannon to parse out individual words. Thomas knelt beside Sienna. He still appeared more puzzled than anything else, but he deftly pocketed the hand cannon while murmuring to his wife. He gently pushed the ruined cake onto the floor, and Tara couldn't help a giggle when a cluster of children led by London darted in for handfuls of the abandoned dessert.

"What is going on here?" demanded a new person. Tara peeked upwards and saw Jack Fairbanks, Thomas's father.

"I don't know, Pa," Thomas said, "but Tara needs a doctor."

"Her name isn't Tara," Tara blurted. "It's Sienna."

"And who are you?" asked Jack Fairbanks.

"That's the coach girl," Thomas said.

Tara stumbled to her feet. "Yes, well, no, I wasn't, but I guess I am now."

"Lying, jealous little cat!" Sienna shouted.

"No," Tara said quietly. "I'm not. I'm Tara Winthrop, and I can prove it."

Feeling a confidence she'd never felt before, Tara plucked out her mama's handkerchief. She didn't have her mama's wind powers, but her mama had given the handkerchief to her for a reason—it wasn't merely a talisman. "Blow, little wind, blow," Tara said firmly and blew on the knot.

The handkerchief jerked out of her hand and untied itself. A breeze swirled through the room, ruffling hair and clothing. Tiny dust motes coalesced into a human form—Mama.

The crowd murmured wonderingly, while Sienna went pale. Thomas patted her shoulder, but his face was creased with worry. Unsurprisingly so, as Tara's mama's wind magic was legendary.

"Greetings, Jack Fairbanks," intoned the ghostly figure. "I entrust my daughter, Tara, to you. Welcome to my family, and may the gods bless our—"

But the rest of her words were lost in the sudden cries of the onlookers. With the words "my daughter", a second cloud of dust motes had swirled into existence, one that bore no resemblance to the woman who had just married Thomas Fairbanks.

"I'm Tara Winthrop," Tara said again. "Sienna, the coach driver, threatened to kill me if I didn't swap places with her. And then threatened to kill me if I told anyone. As you saw, she was willing to shoot me tonight."

Thomas's hand dropped from his wife's shoulder to the pocket holding the hand cannon. He patted it.

The room was utterly quiet. Everybody stared at her. Tara shrugged. "I'll send a telegram to my mama."

Jack cleared his throat and awkwardly knelt on the floor. "Miss Tara, I know you were expecting a younger husband, but will you do me the honour of becoming my wife?"

Tara gaped at him. She would have accepted this proposal only yesterday—even this morning! But things had changed—*she* had changed.

"Thank you, Mr. Fairbanks. I appreciate your kind offer, but I must decline." He made to respond, and she hastily added, "My mama and I won't abandon your town. We'll still help, but that aid and support won't be tied to a marriage with me." She held out a hand. "What do you say . . . Jack?"

He stared at her hand a moment. Finally, he said, "I think that sounds promising, Tara."

He clasped her hand and she helped him to his feet.

It was a clear sunny morning when Tara loaded a small case of her belongings into Falada's storage compartment. She also had a full bin of coal, a hamper of food, and a full canteen plus an extra water jug. London had also helped her ensure that the coach tool kit was complete and in good repair.

She shut the storage compartment door and stretched. Falada

gave a low whistle, and Tara turned to find Jack, London, and Thomas approaching. During the past week they had formed many agreements and arrangements with Tara's mama—and amongst themselves. Relations with Sienna were strained—Tara wasn't sure if her marriage to Thomas would last. But that wasn't her concern. What did concern her was Falada. Even though it could be understood that Sienna had abandoned the coach or given it to Tara, Tara had formally purchased the coach from Sienna.

After discussing it with Falada, they had decided to explore further into the Expanse, mapping the land and gathering information for her mama—for which she was receiving a salary. There were a few more known settlements out here, but she and Falada would hopefully update and add to the general knowledge of the area.

"You sure you don't need an assistant?" London asked.

"Yes, I'm sure," Tara laughed. "I need you here to keep the stables going. Falada will need a proper home when we return."

"And how long will that be?" Jack asked.

Tara shrugged. "That'll depend on what we find. Probably not for a long time. Don't forget about me!" Her light tone pinched a little and the last word squeaked, revealing her anxiety.

"We won't forget," Jack said.

Tara nodded, swallowing a lump in her throat. These would be the last familiar people she'd see in a while—they'd grown into friends and partners in the last week. She'd miss them.

"I better get going then, to take advantage of the daylight," she said.

She hugged London and then Jack and then Thomas.

"Tara," he said, "I'm sorry for—"

"It's okay, Thomas," she said, stepping quickly away from him. "I wasn't ready to get married anyway."

Tara climbed up onto the driver's bench and pressed the buttons on the control box that brought Falada's engines to life. She pulled on goggles and secured her bandana around her nose and mouth.

With a final wave to her friends, Tara steered Falada out of town. The coach whistled enthusiastically and Tara grinned. There was a lot of world out there, and she couldn't wait to see it.

ACKNOWLEDGEMENTS

It takes a lot of people and support to produce a book, and this one is no exception. In fact, *Harvesting Moonshine* has needed more support than some because all these stories were first published individually elsewhere for well over a decade. My network has suffered through these stories not just once, but twice!

First, many thanks to all the wonderful editors with whom I've worked over the years. Selecting my stories for your anthologies and magazines has given me encouragement to keep writing.

Thank you to all my beta readers, my writing group, my friends, and my family. Special thanks to Alison, Krista, Rhonda, and Skyla for pushing, cheerleading, and lighting the way.

Most especially, thanks to Jason and Aurora, who have more than once heard "this story is due at midnight" and, in addition to taking over dinner prep and other chores, have done late-night and last-minute proofreads, and have always provided me with the words that every writer needs: yes, the story is good.

ABOUT THE AUTHOR

M.L.D. Curelas lives in Calgary with two humans and a varying number of guinea pigs. She's been writing since she was small and doesn't appear to be stopping any time soon. Always a glutton for punishment, she is also the publisher at Tyche Books, a Canadian small press that specializes in science fiction, fantasy, and related non-fiction. For more recent works of short fiction, check out *Sherlock Holmes Takes the Stage* or the upcoming *Brave New Girls: Tales of Girls Who Invent and Imagine.*